DAVY FUCHS IN THERAPY

Tony Melange

DAVY FUCHS IN THERAPY

DOUBLE DRAGON

CHAPTER ONE
PART ONE

My name is Davy Fuchs and this is my story. I'm in my therapist's office. He's my fourth therapist. I liked what he said on his website: It stated that he believed the role of a therapist was to help a client explore the meaning one attaches to something. So, impressed with this, I had been writing to him for several months. Because of my schedule, I had not been able to meet him and now; at last, here I am waiting to meet him. Why am I so anxious to meet yet another therapist? I need to know why I attach so much importance to my cock. You see, it nearly got me killed.

"Yes, of course, I'll tell you about myself. I've told you quite a bit in my letters," I said as I eased into a soft leather recliner. It was a bit short for me.

My cognitive behavioral therapist and my pen pal, Dr. P. J. Saulo, recognized my need for more legroom. He pushed a matching footstool toward me. He cleared his throat.

"Start as far back in your memory as you can. Leave out nothing. Include as much detail as possible. Do you understand?"

"Yes," I replied.

"Good. Sometimes it's the little things that become the key to unlocking one's memory bank. What is your earliest clear recollection?"

"Well, little things bring back one and one I've never forgotten. My earliest recollection had to do with my—,"

"Penis, I believe you have indicated many times in your letters."

"Well, yes. Let's see. My first clear recollection takes me back to the Valley."

"The Valley," quizzed PJ?

"Yes, that's what we called the area where my family had its farm."

"I see. Please continue.

"One day we went visiting one of our few neighbors, the Kahlils. The Valley probably should have been called Kahlil Valley since they had three farms. I guess it wasn't because our spread was the largest and supposedly my family had been there for several generations. We even had a creamery. Anyway, Niles Valley had only about a half dozen farms in it. The whole area was a beautiful rural farm country with low-slung hills and gently rolling fields. There was a full-sized creek called Marsh Creek that ran the full length of the valley and eventually dumped into a river. Anyway, it was while we're visiting the Kahlils and of course, I had to use the toilet. I went to their "outhouse." It was hard for me to pee at their place because they didn't have a low hole as my folks did for me.

While I was letting water, the Kahlil girls began bugging me. One was three years older than me; the other was 5 years older. There was a small knothole in the side of the outhouse. I have never forgotten that terrible day. I was so embarrassed. They had

6

been taking turns watching me pee. Suddenly they began their infernal chanting. I was sure the whole world could hear as well as my folks. The chant turned into a screaming, giggling uproar:

We see your pee-wee, pee-wee. Teeny-weenie pee-wee. T'aint no bigger than a bee.

I thought they would never stop their nastiness against my poor defenseless little nub. After all, how big did they think a five-year-old's should be? They were eight and ten. I got even with them when I turned fifteen.

"You raped them?"

"No. I'll get into that a bit later. I want to talk about Peggy. I suppose I can say she was responsible for the second phase of my education. We had moved from the big house to a smaller place at the other end of the valley. It was hard for my mother to manage the big farm with three young boys to care for. My father was in a sanitarium because he had something wrong with his lungs. The big farm was turned over to one of the Kahlils."

"What about Peggy," PJ asked.

"You said you wanted details, didn't you?"

"Well, yes, I did, but your time is about up and I want to end today's session with some degree of understanding."

"It was not an issue to move to another place because we owned most of the houses in the Valley. We owned the house Peggy lived in. It was old; only a faint lingering of paint showed here and there. To get to Peggy's house we had to cross an old bridge over Marsh Creek. Her house made the left side of a square. The country store with its bar was on one side with the church and school on another. Our place of fifteen acres made the fourth side.

"Shortly after we had moved in my mother walked me over the one-lane bridge to her place. Peggy and me were sent out to play so the womenfolk could 'talk'. It was while we were playing in an old shed that my second lesson took place."

"What did she do?"

"She pulled up her dress and shoved her panties down to the ground. The shed had an earthen floor. She told me to look at her bun. I looked. It was a swelled up spot between her legs with a fold down its middle. She told me it was her pee thing and that her uncle said it had to be kept clean so he stuck his finger in it. She said I could feel of it and I wasn't about to do that. She coaxed me to do it. She even tried to take my hand and put it on her pee thing. Then she wanted to see my thing. She wanted to see if it was as big as her uncle's. At age six I wasn't about to do that so I punched her. She ran into the house, told her mother I had pulled her panties down, and had put my finger between her legs. That night I got sent to my room without my supper.

"And you found it repulsive to touch her?"

"Yes. A funny thing happened after that," I said. "Well, not funny as in a joke, but strange."

"And that was?"

8

"Peggy's house burned down. They escaped and disappeared after that. There was quite a bit of speculation about what caused the fire. Folks at the general store said it was set. Now, mind you, I'm not saying it was. Just saying there was some speculations."

"For today we can say you have identified two things that have bothered you: the size of your penis and touching a vagina. You agree with that?"

"Well, yes," I said.

"Good. See you tomorrow at the same time."

As I let myself out, I turned and said to PJ, "Size still matters, doc."

Anyway as I hailed a taxi, I couldn't help but wonder what that conversation had to do with my obsession with sex. I just never seem to get enough. I'll see what tomorrow brings.

***

"Glad to see you came back. Today, let's begin with your name. Has that caused you problems?

"Not early on. But by fifth grade, it was no longer the wenie chant but Davy Fucks."

"And what did you reply to that?"

"I shrugged my shoulders and said, 'Yeah, don't you?'"

"Good come back. I think in of your early letters you indicated you were anxious to start school."

"Yes. I already knew how to read, write, and count. The lesson learned was not the one I had expected. The school was a one-room school. It had eight rows of seats, one for each grade. In the first grade, there was just one other seat besides mine. Row eight was for the eighth grade and there were 4 seats in that row, all occupied. And of course, I had to pee. The "out-house" was in the back of the school building. At recess, we were allowed to go outdoors. It was at that time I headed for the toilet. Someone was already in there. So, I stepped around the corner to relieve myself and as I did I heard giggling. I immediately froze. Then I heard a long drawn out "oh." It came from a little dip in the ground. Slowly, I inched my way closer to see what was going on. One of the "big" boys and a girl were there. He was one of the eighth-graders. He had his pants open and his thing was sticking out. I'd never seen one that big before; not even my brothers' looked that big. The girl was running her hand back and forth on his thing. Then she opened her mouth and he stuck it in there. Her head bobbed back and forth as he pumped it to her.

"Then he looked around and saw me. I ran."

"And that was that?" PJ asked.

"Not quite. Back in class, I had a note passed to me warning me not to say anything or I would be dead meat. I knew he was old enough to hunt. But that wasn't the worst part of my day."

"Not the worst part of your day?"

"My best friend Jimmy came home with me. He was supposed to do that and wait until his mother came to pick him up. After a snack of homemade bread with strawberry jam and a glass of

10

milk, we set off to play. I told Jimmy about what I had seen. His eyes nearly popped out of his head. He suggested we compare. His wasn't as big as mine so he asked me if he could stroke it like the girl did. I hesitated but since he was my best friend, I agreed. He pushed it up and down. Suddenly I peed and it went all over his clothes. Jimmy started yelling at me. My mother heard him and came to see what was wrong. Jimmy told her I peed on him. No matter how I protested, I was sent off to my room and told never to do that again. Jimmy and me weren't friends after that. Later when he was old enough he got drafted and got killed in Korea. When his folks had a funeral for him, I didn't go. We weren't friends anymore."

"Do you feel guilty about not going to Jimmy's funeral?"

"No, there was no point in me going."

"Anything else during this early period of your life you remember?"

"There is. The reason I remember is I thought I was going to get killed," I said.

"Killed," PJ questioned.

"It was on a Saturday. I dashed across the highway to the school. I liked going there to swing in an old tire tied on a heavy rope. Next to the school was a large semi-wooded area that had hickory nut trees. Squirrels were not the only ones who liked hickory nuts. Tiring of the swing I wandered over to the hickory tree grove. I had noticed the Gypsies had arrived. They always stopped there on their way to wherever they were

11

going. I liked watching them and their trucks with colorful little houses attached to the truck bed. There were always lots of colors even their clothing. Additionally, they always left a pile of stuff when they moved on. I liked checking that out. I noticed a boy about my brother's age and a girl slip out from behind one of the trucks.

Hand in hand they ran across the field and ended up beneath the very tree I was in. She pulled off her clothes and placed them on the ground in a neat pile. He did the same thing. She had long black hair that tumbled down over her large breasts and a dark patch of hair between her legs. His hang down was standing straight out. She knelt and opened her mouth and he shoved it in. He grabbed her by the hair and pulled her closer to him. His hang-down disappeared in her mouth. Suddenly he began to shove back and forth. And then he stopped. He let her head go, she then lay down on their clothes, spread her legs and he mounted her. I dropped some of the nuts I had put in my pocket. She opened her eyes and saw me. I heard her say "Look!" and he turned. By then I was climbing down out of the tree as fast as I could. He jumped up and caught me by my shirt as I hit the ground.

Hanging on to me, he bent down and picked up a large knife, pulled his arm back, ready to slit my throat. The girl jumped up, put her hand on his arm, and said, "Don't. He's just a little kid."

He let go of me and I ran as fast as I could. That was the last time I went there. I realized girls were okay. At least that one, she saved my life."

12

"Do you feel these early encounters with human sexuality laid the basis for your unquenchable sexual thirst?" PJ said.

"I never thought about it; not in those terms anyway," I replied. "My throat is quite dry. May I have a drink?" *Finally, I thought, we're getting to the issue.*

"That summer we moved into town. It was a large house with a wide porch facing the street. The house was big enough so each of us kids could have a bedroom of our own. There was a separate garage for the car. A large two-acre field was behind the house and joined a road that connected to the town's park and swimming pool. An old lady lived on one side of our house and an old couple lived on the other. There were no other kids my age or my brothers' ages around really close by. Anyway, unlike most kids, I was anxious for school to start."

"Well, that is different," PJ said.

PART TWO

At the end of August, we moved into town and that was different. The house was a large brown building with a wide porch across its front. There was a separate building my father called a garage. I guess town folks didn't call them sheds as we did on the farm. Speaking of the farm, my folks simply closed it up. In the new house, each of my brothers and me had our separate rooms; whereas, at the small farm we slept in a large partially unfinished room. Behind the new house was two acres of field that connected to the next street that ran by the town park. Our house sat on a knoll and overlooked the rest of the street. I remember my mother saying that it was good to have some acreage and being close to the park since we were used to large hunks of land to roam. She had no idea what that would do for me.

"I had a little over a mile to walk to school. My mother had walked me there and back the day before school officially opened. I didn't tell her I knew a shortcut over the hill. Two of the kids that lived one street up from my house had shown it to me. It was warm and I decided to take the short cut home. It would bring me by the park up from our house.

Some distance along the trail I found a bare-ass naked boy lying on top of a half-naked girl. His butt was going up and down like crazy. I recognized them as been second-graders like me. I stopped to watch."

I heard myself saying, "What are you two creeps doing?"

"Fucking! What's it look like?" the boy grunted.

So that's what it's called. Fucking. I thought.

"And that was when you learned the common name for sexual intercourse," PJ said.

"Yes. I remember I sat down to watch. It didn't seem to bother them in the least. He was sure doing a lot of pushing up and down. Suddenly she spoke up.

"Enough. It's my turn now."

With that, he got up, his cock was straight out and looked hard. He then lay down on his back and she squatted down on him, grunted once, and then began to slide up and down on his cock. They were so involved. I don't think she even saw me as she looked right at me. I got bored and walked home.

"How did you feel about what you watched?"

"Well, the fact is, I felt pretty ignorant. I felt I was totally lacking."

Sometime in October, my folks took on what they called a hired girl. She was from the valley. She was a big girl, especially in the chest area. Her job was to help with the meals, do the laundry, and clean the house. And when necessary she was to babysit me. Her name was Amy. One night my folks and two brothers went out for the evening.

Amy decided to read to me so we sat on the davenport in the living room. The story was about King Arthur. I liked the way she read. A half-hour later, my middle brother, Billy walked in.

15

"I told you I'd be back," he said looking at Amy.

"I'm reading Davy a story. You want to sit and listen?" She giggled.

I didn't see anything funny. Billy sat down close to Amy. She continued to read and he slid his hand down her neck to her large tits. He squeezed one, then he unbuttoned her dress and her tits tumbled out. Billy squeezed first one and then the other. He rubbed each nipple between his thumb and forefinger. I was surprised to see them pop out.

"And did that excite you?" PJ asked.

"No. Amy kept on reading as if nothing happened. Her tits began to heave up and down. Her legs opened. Billy slipped his hand under her dress. Amy's mouth opened and she stopped reading. I heard a whispered 'yes.' Billy began kissing her tits and then licking the very pink nubs. Her breathing increased as Billy kept his hand very busy under her dress. I was completely fascinated. Before I was aware of it, I was rubbing one of her large tits. Her closed eyes opened wide. Billy said, "Be gentle, Davy." Amy giggled.

"It's nice Billy. Feels really nice," I said.

"Want to feel of something even nicer, Davy?" Billy asked.

"Now, Billy, don't," Amy said.

I could tell she didn't mean it. I got down and stood between her open legs. I could see a mass of brown hair with a pink slit.

"Go ahead, Davy, put her hand there, and rub and slip your middle finger in."

Haltingly, I laid my hand on her. It was warm and soft. I did what Billy told me to do and slid my middle finger into the pink slit. It was very warm and moist. Billy pushed my whole hand in. It felt like velvet, smooth, warm, and wet. I thought she was peeing on me.

"You feel really nice, Amy," I said. "You're warm all over."

Amy giggled and Billy laughed.

"You want to see something, Amy?" I asked.

"Sure, Davy, I want to see something," Amy snickered.

As she continued her sprawled legs, Billy was working his hand in her thick brown hair. I reached over, jerked down Billy's zipper, and before he could say anything I had his underwear down and his prick was standing up thick and rigid. It was bigger than any of the others I had seen. With a quick movement, he had his belt off and his pants down to the floor. He bent down, pulled a little package from his pants pocket. I thought it was a pack of matches. I was surprised when he opened it up and pulled a round thing out of it.

"What's that?" I asked.

"A rubber," Billy replied.

I watched with total fascination as he slipped it over his huge throbbing cock.

"What's it for?" I asked.

"Prevents babies," Amy said.

I was taken back by that.

Billy put his hands under her butt and pulled her up to him, then with one hand he took his rigid

"Didn't you tell your other psychiatrists about these early experiences?" PJ asked.

"No. They never asked," I replied.

PART THREE

"So, what happened next? Did Billy and Amy continue to let you watch them have sex?" PJ asked.

"Amy was let go. My mother said she got lazy and wasn't taking care of the house, and meals were late. The World War was raging throughout Europe. Then the Japanese got involved. My brothers enlisted. The older one went into the army. Billy had to have our father sign approval so he could enlist. He joined the Navy. It seemed everyone got involved. It was time to be patriotic. My mother decided to take a job in a local defense factory and my father got involved with moving supplies for the troops. Booth took their turns on air-watch. Sometimes I went with them to the tower on top of the local hotel. I could identify planes by their shape and learned to recognize the sound of their motors.

My folks rented out one of the bedrooms to a red-haired man who was a 4-f-er. I was told that it meant he didn't pass a physical exam to get drafted into the military. He worked at a local milk plant. One day he came home early and had a woman with him. He told me it was his sister. They went upstairs to his bedroom and shut the door. I thought that was strange. I quietly tip-toed upstairs and listened at his door. No sound. Then I heard a grunt and the bed began to squeak. Being curious, I slowly opened the bedroom door. Both were naked and he was on top of her with his butt going up and down. *They're fucking*, I thought.

Since I was used to being an observer, I went on in. He certainly wasn't a big as Billy and she didn't have big tits like Amy. When he finished, he sat up on the edge of the bed. That's when he saw me. He was really mad. He swore at me and then slapped me so hard it knocked me down. I ran to my room and locked the door. I heard them running down the steps. I looked out my window and saw them get into his car and drive off.

When my mother came home and found me locked in my room she demanded to know why. When I opened the door she could see I had been crying and my eye was black.

"What happened to you? Why are you crying? Goodness, your eye is black. Have you been in a fight at school?" my mother said.

I told her I was in the renter's room and she wanted to know I was there. When I told her I was watching the naked lady on the bed with the man on top of her and the renter slapped me

"Oh, my God!"

She then went downstairs, got some ice from an ice tray, brought it back up to my room, and had me hold on my eye. I heard her in the renter's room. She slammed dresser drawers and a closet door. She dragged his suitcase downstairs and put it out on the front porch. She told my father when he got home. That's when they got into an argument. She wanted a full-time hired girl. He thought it was silly to have a babysitter for me. My mother won the argument. I agreed with him but changed my mind later.

The next day when I got home from school a girl was sitting on the steps of the front porch. She was pretty.

"Hi, my name is Sally. You must be Davy. I'm the new housekeeper."

She talked easy as I let her in. I liked her. *I bet Billy will like her even more.*

My mother was impressed with Sally because she had completed everything on the list of things she wanted to be done. She even had our dinner started and my father liked that. Later that night, after everyone had gone to bed, I left my room and sipped into Sally's room.

"You lonesome, Sally?" I asked

"A little," she replied.

"Mind if I visit for a while?"

"Not at all," she said as she pulled back the covers.

She smelled nice and I told her so. I did a lot of talking and eventually fell asleep. That morning my mother wanted to know why I was in Sally's room.

"Gee, mom, I thought she might be lonesome. You know, her first time being away from home," I said.

She laughed and said, "Well, just don't make yourself a pest, you hear."

I knew what I was going to make.

That night was bath night for me. I got scrubbed twice a week. Rest of the time I was expected to wash myself. My parents were going out to one of their card parties. My brothers were at a basketball game. Sally was left with the job of supervising my bath. She came into the bathroom to check on how I was doing. I was just getting out of the tub. For some reason, I felt embarrassed and she must have noticed that because she had me turn around so she could dry my back.

She was gentle. The first thing I knew she had me turned around, facing her.

"Lift your arms, Davy," she said.

I did. It tickled me as she dried under my arms. Slowly the towel moved down my chest and then to my belly. She was enjoying toweling me. Then she had my cock and balls in her hands. She dried my privates for quite a while.

"Get your pj's on and come downstairs and I'll have a slice of cake and a glass of milk for you," Sally said.

I sat at the kitchen table. She leaned over me to pour me a glass of milk. I felt her tits rub against my head. I leaned back a bit further.

"If you want, I'll read you another chapter out of your favorite book. You can get in bed with me until your folks get home," Sally said.

Upstairs in her bedroom, I watched her undress. Her body was soft white. I noticed her tits. They weren't really big like Amy's but they were nice. Each was capped with a pink nipple. She pulled the covers back, slipped into bed with me, and turned off the light.

I guess there's no story. I rolled over and put an arm over her.

"I hope you never leave here, Sally, I said as I snuggled my head on her shoulder."

"That's nice of you to say that. You do like me, don't you?"

"Yes, and besides you're pretty," I replied.

"You wouldn't be looking for another piece of cake, now would you?" She teased.

As I assured her that was not the case, I slowly brought my hand down to one of her breasts and gently rubbed it. Since she did not object, I continued a slow massage. Her nipple firmed. I leaned in a bit closer and gently rolled my tongue over her firm nipple as I slid my hand down her belly. It, like her tit, was smooth.

"You feel real nice, Sally," I whispered. "I like the way you feel."

"That's nice. I'm glad, Davy."

My hand wandered into her patch of hair. Instinctively, she closed her legs but I kept my hand right where it was. She didn't move it away. Slowly I rubbed her patch with circles just as I had watched Billy do to Amy. Her legs opened. I shoved my finger into her slit. Then three fingers. She gasped as I continued to busy my fingers. She got moist and her breathing got faster.

I inched my way down between her legs and began kissing her open slit. She moaned. I licked my way back up to her firm tits and as I did I pushed against her patch. My young stick suddenly hardened. I was thrilled as it slid into her. It was moist, warm, and all velvety. I realized she was saying something.

"What?" I panted.

"Slowly, Davy, slowly."

I tried to slow down, but the excitement I was feeling exploded. For a few minutes, I just laid on her, not moving.

"You're a naughty boy, Davy, doing that bad thing to me," Sally whispered.

"Did it feel good?"

"Well, yes it did, but—,"

"Then it wasn't bad or naughty. Anything that feels good can't be bad," I said.

She giggled and hugged me as she said, "You better go to your room."

"Okay," I said, as I rubbed her patch. "You're wonderful, Sally."

And I continued to think so; at least for a short while.

"So, you stopped having sex with Sally?" PJ asked.

"Yes. She began acting queer. She pinched me, hard, scratched me with her fingernails, and then tried slapping me. I told her to knock it off. She didn't ask me to slip into her bed with her anymore. One day, when I got home from school she was gone. After that, there were no more hired, girls."

"Did her leaving upset you?" PJ said.

"Actually, no. The War was raging on. I was in sixth grade and busy writing my first play. That's when I met Charlene."

"Tell me about her."

"Well, her mother and my parents were friends. We had been invited to Charlene's house for dinner.

Afterward, the adults played poker. It was then that I learned how to play strip poker with Charlene and her older sister, Dottie who was an eighth-grader. I nearly lost my pants. Anyway, Charlene got bored and wanted to go outside. We decided to go over to the lumber yard that was a block away. A small creek divided the yard from the railroad tracks. We crossed over the creek using a small bridge. She led me along the creek, over a stone wall, and into a large wooden crate. One side opened like a door."

"Come in, Davy," she said.

I followed her. She pulled out a pack of cigarettes, offered me one, took one for herself. She used a lighter. I puffed away.

"Don't puff so much. Go slow," Charlene said.

I remembered hearing that before.

"You want someone to think this place is on fire?"

"I slowed down. I even got a bit dizzy. Eventually, we butted our smokes. It was right after that that things suddenly changed."

"What changed?"

"She pulled up her dress. She was naked. I was more interested now; more than I had been with Peggy a couple of years ago. I noticed she didn't have any real hair, just some fuzz. Her closed slit was visible."

"Go ahead, Davy. Put your hand there," Charlene whispered.

I did as I was told. She felt smooth, almost soft. Gently I began to rub her.

"Drop your pants and put your thing on me," Charlene said.

"Don't think I better, Char," I replied.

"You chicken?"

"Of course not. Don't be dumb," I replied.

"Then do it. Put it on me and hold it there."

"No."

"I'll tell your folks you were smoking. Two other boys have put their things on me. Come on, Davy, don't be such a baby."

"Tell me, Char, did these other boys shove their dicks in there?"

"What do you mean?"

"Want me to show you?"

"Only, if you do what I want."

"Okay, lay down, spread your legs."

I began to rub her slit. Gently at first, gradually increasing the pressure, I slid my finger into her crack. She gasped and opened her eyes.

"What the hell you doing?" She said.

"Showing you how to screw. That's what you want, isn't it?"

I continued to work my finger and unlike Sally, she didn't get moist. I raised up, pulled my pants down, and took out my very stiff poker. She was amazed at its size.

"The other boys' things didn't look like that," she said.

Slowly I eased down on her, making sure I had my very hard cock ready. I shoved full force and she yelled. I kept shoving downward until I was finally all the way in. It must have hurt because she

27

continued to whimper. I increased my speed. Suddenly she was moist. I glided in and out easily. She put her arms around me and hugged me. She was liking it. I got very sensitive as I pounded it into her. The delight subsided and I removed myself from her now very swollen slit.

"My god, Davy, no one has ever done that to me before. It hurt at first then felt real good. You can do that do me any time you want," Charlene whispered as I pulled up my pants.

"I was very pleased with myself."

"Pleased with yourself? I thought you already had sex with Sally," PJ said.

"It was my first with someone my age," I replied.

"Of course. If you don't mind I'd like to change our procedure. Our session has run well over the time limit and it's my dinner time. Will you join me?"

Hmm. Wonder what he wants. It certainly isn't the standard protocol. "Do you always invite your clients to dinner?" I said after a long pause.

"No, I don't. It's just that you remind me so much of my grandson."

"Grandson?"

"Yes, he committed suicide some twenty years ago."

"Sorry to hear that. What . . ."

"I am over it and do not need to talk about it. If you want to join me for dinner I need to call my housekeeper and have her set out another plate."

28

I agreed and that began a long relationship until he died at the age of eighty. Dr. Paul J. Saulo became my mentor and best friend.

We left the first-floor office via an old bird-cage elevator. This was the first time I noted PJ used a cane. We exited into a very large room whose walls were lined with floor-to-ceiling bookshelves; all lined with books. From there, he had me follow him into another large room with three walls mahogany paneled walls. The fourth wall was a huge glass window that offered a spectacular view of the city's nightscape. The sun's last evening glow completed the magic.

A long table with only two place settings commanded the center of the room. I was the only guest. Beef Wellington, assorted vegetables were complemented with a marvelous vintage red wine. Desert was a flaming something or other. After dinner, he escorted me to another large room with glass doors that opened onto a veranda. We sat, quietly watching the moon rise. Brandy was brought by the maid. I remained quiet; not wishing to intrude on my host's private thoughts. He seemed miles away; most likely years.

He reached over to a silver box, opened it, and handed me a long thin cigar.

"My own brand. Had them specially made for me in Havana."

Even though I was not a regular smoker of cigars, those I had were okay. This one was very different. Its smoke was sweet, mild, and added to the pleasantness of the evening. After a few puffs I began to feel wonderful; easy contentment settled over me. My whole inner being was clothed in a new richness. My mind felt free and expanded into a rainbow of divine thought. I vaguely saw my soul float upward—upward to Zeus. All was well with the world and with my soul. I was in reverie.

Somewhere out of the fog of my mind, I heard him call my name.

"Davy?" PJ quietly said.

"What?" I mumbled.

"You fell asleep. How do you feel?"

Shaking myself, I replied, "Okay. Oh, man! I'm sorry about falling asleep, Doc. What time is it?"

"No problem. It's eight o'clock. Do you feel up to continuing your story?"

"Sure, just up from my house was the town's park. Our property ended at the park. I'd heard rumors from some of the older kids that it was a lover's paradise. Wanting to find out for myself, I began making nightly sorties to the park."

"Your parents didn't object to your doing this?"

"They didn't know. I waited until they were asleep. The roof to the back porch was just beneath my bedroom window. Next to one side of the roof was a tree. I quietly opened my window, eased down to the roof, and climbed down the tree. I made sure I left the window open so I could get back in."

"What time of night was this? Weren't you afraid?"

"Generally, it was around eleven o'clock. Because I didn't take a flashlight with me and because there were only three streetlights in the park, I didn't see much, except once."

"Tell me about that."

"A car was parked beneath one of the streetlights which was located at the entrance to the town's swimming pool. I slipped under the gate, climbed up the steps to the top of the pool. From there I good see directly into a parked car. I don't know how long they had been there but they began to undress each other. I watched as she sat on his lap. Gradually she began moving up and down. He softly groaned. He massaged her breasts as she leaned forward and kissed him over and over. Her speed increased and he bucked. This time she moaned. Their movement rocked their car. And then they were quiet. She lifted herself up from his lap; he coughed, opened the car door, and threw something on the ground."

"And did watching excite you? PJ said.

"Well, yes. But when he opened the car door, I thought he saw me. So I didn't get a chance to play with myself because he took his time before he shut the car door. Then I realized he was putting on another rubber."

"And that was the end of that?"

"Well No. If I was so heated up I would have felt his presence."

"The man in the car came after you?"

No. I eased myself down the cement stairway and rounded a corner of the pool. That's when he grabbed me."

"Who grabbed you?"

31

"As he dragged me away from the light I caught a glimpse of his face. It was Larry, my neighbor."

"Keep quiet. Don't make a sound. You hear?" Larry said as he removed his hand from my mouth.

I nodded my head. He was bigger than me. Older, too. At least eighteen since he didn't go to school. Suddenly, he shoved me to the ground. Before I could roll away, he clutched my dick and balls, ripped open my pants, and had me in his mouth. His tongue flew around my dick as his lips slid up and down bringing me to a full hard erection. He swallowed me as I shoved upward.

"You had better not say anything about this. If you do, you're dead meat. You understand?" Larry said as he stood and pulled me up. He was breathing hard, bent his head down, and kissed me. He disappeared into the darkness. I wiped my mouth with the back of my hand.

The quiet of the early morning was broken by a sharp crack; then a second one. I ran.

The local police stopped at my house. They wanted to know if they heard anything. I listened in. That was when I learned that there was a murder-suicide at the park."

"What about Larry? Did you ever see him again?" PJ asked

"No," I replied.

"What, if anything, did your other therapist say about this incident?"

32

"You're the first one I've told about that. Fact is, there's a lot I've never told before."

"I appreciate the confidence. Did you continue to see Charlene?"

"Only once more. We were playing up in her attic. I got her to drop her pants and lay down. I got in between her legs and began to lick her slit. She began to squirm. I reached down, opened my pants, and was just about to stick it to her when her mother opened the attic door and called that lunch was ready. Years later, I heard she was working the streets in Chicago. Mind if I refill that snifter with your brandy?"

"Help yourself. Pour one for me while you are at it," PJ said. "Anything else you want to talk about that you remember before your teen years?"

"It's after midnight, PJ. I apologize for keeping you up."

PART FOUR

By thirteen I had started to tall-up. My feet were getting bigger and my voice cracked at the oddest times causing a flood of laughter and embarrassing me. My relatives said I was growing up and would soon be interested in girls. Then they would snicker. I chuckled at their assumption. If they only knew.

Not sure who blabbed but the word got around that I was a real stud even though my public hair had not grown in. That worried me a bit. I checked every night and every morning. One morning I realized I had a mass of blond hair.

I turned an old tool shed into a special place. It was located behind our garage. It didn't have a window. I fixed the door so I could lock it from the inside while I was in there. I had a box for a table, a shelf, and burlap bags on the floor for carpet. One early fall Saturday I was in my Club House, that's what I had begun calling it when there was a slight tapping at the door. I peeked through a crack in the door. Diane Weaver stood there.

I opened the door and asked her what she wanted. Without answering me, she brushed past me and walked in, turned, and shut the door.

"Hi, Davy. What you doing?" Diane said.

"Just fooling around."

"I hear you fool around real good. That true?"

I looked at her as she leaned back against the closed door; mouth slightly open and eyes partially closed. She looked silly as hell. Instinct told me what she wanted. I moved in closed to her, put my arm above her head, and brushed my lips across her cheek.

"Yeah, I fool around," I said as I brushed my hand across a nipple. It was firm.

"Really," she whispered as I leaned into her. Kissing her, I slid my hand down to her cunt. She pushed against my hand. I began a gentle rubbing. I realized she didn't have on any underwear. I pulled her dress up and let my fingers do the walking as they slide into her firm mons. I didn't shove my finger in and out. I had learned to move it around, to curl it as I teased. Diane's breathing quickened it."

I flattened my hand against her swollen clit and squeezed. Diane gasped.

"Fuck me, Davy. Fuck me!"

Easing her down to the floor, I slipped my pants down, took my throbbing cock in my hand, and tapped her cunt with it; teasing her until her little nub popped. Slowly, ever so slowly I eased my hard cock into her gaping clit. With one shove it was up to its hilt. I slide my hands under her, lifted her as I leaned back, making sure my cock stayed in place. She realized she had full reign with my club and ride it up and down she did. Finally, gasping for air, she stopped, dropped her head on my shoulder, and said, "Oh, Davy, Davy."

I wanted more but she said she had to get home. Without saying anything more, she dressed and left.

"Did you see her again?" PJ asked.

"No. I guess she was just collecting experience same as me."

35

"I see, and what came next?"

By my mid-thirteen, I had a full crop of blond pubic hair that now nestled my even bigger club. My voice had settled down to a reasonable baritone. My shoulders had broadened and I had gotten longer-legged. A few parties sprung up here and there and I was always invited. Spin-in-the-bottle was the game of choice. I thought it was silly but most of the time I enjoyed the girls grabbing my cock. Once, one of the guys did that. The game changed to Spot-light.

"Spotlight?" I've not heard that one before," PJ said.

"Lights are turned off, there's some scrambling. One person is giving a flashlight. At the count of 100, the flashlight is turned on. Whoever it spots, and if they are making out, they are "it" and take the flashlight. As soon as the lights went out I always got grabbed and I'm sure sometimes it was the guys. They'd seen me naked after gym class. Most of the time there was just a lot of heavy petting but once in a while a couple would be humping one another."

"I see," PJ said.

"Days passed into weeks and I had gotten another year older. At fourteen I took up golf and tennis and spent my summer days at the local country club. Both games furthered my education."

"And how is that?"

PART FIVE

Carol was about five feet tall, mountains for boobs, slender in the hips. She had long black hair that hung down her back. Her eyes were as dark as her hair but showed a decided deviltry. She was sixteen. She always wore tight blouses, tennis skirts, and shoes. She saw me watching her playing tennis with the club pro. After their last match, she walked over to me.

"You want to learn to play?" Carol said.

"Sure, you going to teach me?"

I knew she had had lessons from one of the professional women tennis players in Coral Gables. I had trouble with my serve. She would stop, come to me, and show me. Sometimes she would put her arms around my shoulders and swing them. One day we were having a good set and she jumped to smash one down her large tits popped out. They were quite the sight. She had trouble pulling herself together. Being the gentleman that I am, I went to her rescue. I pulled back her blouse, unfastened her bra, and then very gently pulled it up and refastened it. I managed to let my fingers linger just a bit. Her firm nipples brushed my hand. She was embarrassed.

It's okay, Carol. No big deal that your strap broke," I said.

"And that was that?" PJ asked.

"We made a date to play golf the next day. She would pick me up in her car. She arrived promptly at eight o'clock. It was a ten-mile ride to the country club. Since we were both members, we had no green fees to pay. We played the first nine and was coming around for eighteen. A woman was about to tee off so we sat down on a bench and waited. It was my dentist's wife, Lynn Lions. She was drunk. I nearly flipped. Carol jumped up and yelled.

Lynn made a hole-in-one. She didn't realize what she had done. Once she was out of range, we teed off. I would make my hole-in-one on the seventh."

"Unbelievable. You were, what fourteen, and made a hole-in-one? Good god, I've played golf for forty years and never even came close," PJ said.

"Well, that's not exactly what I am talking about. Carol teed off first and made a perfect shot. She would be on in two. I deliberately drove my ball into the nearby woods."

"Damn," I yelled in feigned anger.

"Hey, don't sweat it. We'll just go and find your ball. Come on," Carol said as she headed for the woods.

She's going to find more than one ball.

I found the ball, picked it up, and hid it under another shrub, just a short distance from our golf bags. I had brought them into the woods with me on the pretext that we didn't need someone to rip them off. After poking around for a while I suggested we take a break and flopped down on the soft pine floor of the woods. It was thick and smelled nice. She flopped down beside me.

I rolled over on my side and looked at her. Her breasts were something. I could see the nipples

38

through her blouse and I was sure they were winking at me.

"Carol, don't move. A big spider is crawling on you," I said.

"Where is it? Hurry! Get it off of me."

"There," I said as I slipped my hand under her blouse. She didn't have a bra on. I gently rubbed each breast.

"Oh," Carol said.

"Oops," I said. "Didn't mean to scare you."

I unbuttoned her blouse, spread it open, and gently tongued each breast. Her beautiful pink nipples firmed. She softly groaned as I sucked first one then the other. Slowly I traced my finger down her abdomen and on down in between her slightly parted legs and ever so gently rubbed her furry mons. I eased my middle finger in her slit. She gasped and began to squirm.

"I thought you wanted to play golf," Carol whispered.

"I do. I got a club and two balls. You got the cup. Let's tee off," I whispered.

With that, I had her skirt up and was kissing her fast swelling mons. Her legs opened as my tongue worked her.

"Davy, oh Davy. Please," she moaned as I fingered her.

I dropped my pants below my knees and set my large throbbing cock free. With one steady shove, I was all the way into her. As I kissed her sweet lips, I began a systematic assault upon her unused clit. First, a stroke to the left; then one to the right, and a thrust down the middle. Her breathing roared by my ear as I went down her center and reamed. She gasped. Small animal sounds came from her throat; her wetness increased and she gurgled into her first man created orgasm.

"And you, how did you feel?" PJ Saulo asked.

"As for me, I was filled with a new and genuine sense of delight. She was such a willing partner; the smell of the pines and the beautiful day increased my desire beyond and pleasure point I had previously experienced.

"What happened next?"

"Well, I increased my thrust as I slammed into her. Carol began to thrash beneath me and the more she did so, the faster I drove my thick cock into her My hot juice filled her dripping cunt as I collapsed on her. We both lay still as our heavy breathing subsided. I gently kissed her and then began kissing her mountainous tits. I rolled their nipples with my tongue and they firmed. Her passion grew and I crawled up and over those large tits and offered my huge erection to her open lips. Eagerly she should me, took me in, and caressed my cock with her warm moist tongue. She worked her way down my shaft and licked my balls, slowing taking each one in her mouth and then she licked her way back to the top of my bulging cock and ran her tongue around its head. I was ecstatic. I felt the building pressure and changed my position so I had a straight shot into her open mouth. With one gulp she swallowed me and I exploded. I waited until the spasm stopped and then extracted myself from her throat.

"You like my kind of golf?" I laughed as I helped her up.

Carol giggled as she pulled herself together, brushing the pine needles from her skirt. I wrapped my arms around her, kissed her. We agreed to golf again the next day. Unfortunately, I didn't make it the next day.

"Why not?" PJ asked.

"My parents and I left that morning for our annual month-long vacation to the lake. We drove for two days, late into the night of each. We parked along the road so my father could sleep for a couple of hours. On the third day, we arrived at our camp. Once the boat and foodstuffs were unloaded we had something to eat and headed out onto the lake with our boat. It was while we were at the camp that I had the most exquisite experience of my life; the one that started me on the long quest that has finally brought me to you."

"Fascinating," PJ said as he stifled a yawn.

"That part of my story will have to wait until tomorrow. I'm really tired and so are you."

"Forgive me. I didn't realize the lateness of the hour. You will stay here. Come, I'll show you to your room. We'll continue after breakfast."

CHAPTER TWO
PART ONE

My room at PJ's place was very large. A quick guess put it at about thirty feet in length. A large marble-faced fireplace dominated one wall. The center wall had two large glass doors that emptied onto a balcony. The other wall held a massive, canopied bed. The fourth wall was floor to ceiling bookcases. A long oriental rug lay on each side of the bed. On each side of the bed, on the wall were old gas lights that had been converted to electricity. A beautifully carved wooden desk sat a discrete distance from the bookcases. It contained a desk lamp with a heavy dark green shade.

As I began to undress, a light tap at my door. It opened and a middle-aged man dressed in black walked in. He was carrying a small silver tray with stemmed crystal glass and a small crystal decanter.

"Dr. Saulo thought you might enjoy a warmed Cognac before retiring," the man said as he sat the tray down on a marble-topped nightstand. After a quick shower, I sipped the Cognac, turned off the light, and rolled into bed.

I slept very well and very late. When I came downstairs it was ten o'clock and my host had already had breakfast. I was served by the same man who had brought me the Cognac. He brought eggs Mornay, hard rolls, fresh fruit, and coffee. As I was finishing my coffee, the same man reappeared.

"Dr. Saulo would like you to join him in the solarium. If you will follow me."

"What is your name?" I asked as I shoved my chair back from the table.

"Joseph, sir."

"Thank you, Joseph."

Joseph led me down a long hall and into a large room made entirely of glass. An abundance of flowering and non-flowering plants filled the area; yet, there was space for two chairs with a table between them. The sun felt good.

"Plants are great healers, you know," PJ said. "And a good morning to you. Did you sleep well?"

"Yes, thank you."

"Do you feel up to continuing this morning?"

"Yes, yes I do."

"Good. Would you have another cup of coffee as we begin our session?"

He poured each of a cup of coffee from a silver carafe. As was his apparent custom, we sat in silence while we sipped our coffee. Once again, he offered a cigar. Its richness filled me with continued contentment. And again I felt the luxury of warm freedom bathe me in exquisite ease. My whole being relaxed and I felt one with the world.

"Well, Davy, you left off with your family's trip here to Canada," PJ said.

"PJ, you never told me what your initials stand for," I said as I stalled a bit in going on with my story.

"Paul Jonathan. Paul after my father and Jonathan after my grandfather," PJ said as he blew a ring of cigar smoke in the air.

I took that to mean I better get on with my story. We lived in tents on a large man-made lake in Quebec Province. It covered 250 miles. It was created in the 1920s when Mercier Dam was built. The whole area was a pristine gorgeous wonderland. I had taken to exploring and rowing about on the lake. I enjoyed the exercise and it helped my bodybuilding.

On one of my many rowing days, I stopped by one of the many small islands, anchored the boat, stripped off my clothes, and drove into the water. August was warm and the water was a delight. After a few more dives off my boat, I rowed to shore, pulled the boat up on the sandy beach, turned it over, and then began to walk to the center of the island. There, there was a small clearing, a secluded spot I had discovered on a previous visit. I planned to just lay there in the sun, enjoy my privacy, and especially enjoy my body.

I didn't see them immediately. Good luck prevented me from barging in on them. A tall slender boy and girl, both naked, stood in the very center of the small clearing. Both were Indians. He stood stall in front of her, showing his very stiff masculine pride. Doe-eyed she followed his strong young body wither her fingers; slowly reaching his balls and gently cupped them in both hands. Their beautiful nut-brown skin was radiant. She was so graceful with her long black hair flowing over exquisite breasts. Neither spoke.

"How did you feel watching them?" PJ asked.

"Guilty."

"Guilty?"

"Yes, for watching, no spying on them. I felt like an intruder on something very special, a beautiful thing. And yet, it was a feeling I had not experienced before. It was their total beauty that held me, making me a prisoner to continued observation. It was the image of total oneness they showed, oneness with the Universe itself.

I was so hypnotized by this couple. So much so that I had completely forgotten I still was naked and that I had my clothes rolled up in a bundled tucked under my arm. I dropped them to the ground and sat down on them. There was just enough sun to further the pleasure I was experiencing.

He reached out and very gently with the tip of his fingers touched each of her perfect breasts. He traced a finger over each several times and during this neither spoke, each holding the other's gaze and never blinking. Then without ceremony, he slipped his arm around her demure waist and pulled her into to him. I thought he was going to kiss her, but instead, he held her close, his stiff cock pressing against her. They wrapped themselves around each other and folded themselves into one another. Hanging suspended in time—unending—a perfect live sculpture true to the Greek tradition of physical perfection. He began caressing her, stroking her long black hair. He handled her like a delicate flower. Then they separated. His maleness showed itself, firm, long, and thick. She openly admired him. I wanted to move closer but I was afraid of being seen and I didn't want to spoil such a splendid moment.

Without a word or sign, he sat down on the warm sand, crossed his legs beneath him, and with perfect control bend back until he touched the earth beneath him. His crossed legs formed a base and his head, the tip. He arched his back and his stiff cock became a pivotal point. He was so still I could not even tell if he was breathing.

"Then what?" PJ said as he poured another cup of coffee.

"The girl went to him and slowly sat down his protuberant war club. She stretched her legs and locked her feet under his arms and laid back until her head rested on the ground. Neither moved after that."

"Are you saying they died?" PJ said.

"I waited for a while and then crept closer. I was careful not to make a sound. Their eyes were closed. Once I was in the clearing I went up to them. I bent down on my knees and looked at them. She was well planted on his cock. The only sign of life was a very slow movement of their chests. It was a lover trance—a total union of body and mind. I was filled with a new understanding about total surrender to another and I was overjoyed.

I'm not sure at what point I became aware that he was looking at me. His dark eyes filled with anger. He was about to speak but I quickly pressed a finger to his lips. It was strange. He seemed to read my mind and sensing no personal harm or threat from me the anger disappeared. I felt him question my intrusion; yet, he did not speak. He noticed my nakedness and openly looked at my enlarged cock. His eyes widened and I sensed a hint of wishful admiration and then it just as quickly faded.

Without any hesitation, I laid down beside them, pressing close to his thigh. I reached out and touched him. His skin was smooth. I made small circles on his flat stomach and with each completion of a circle; I came closer to his rich black public hair. He watched me all the time I was doing this. I touched the base of his implanted hard shaft. I felt its life beat. He turned his head ever so slightly toward me and smiled. I knew I was welcome. Their pleasure would be mine also.

I continued to play at his base. He gave me an even warmer and broader smile as his acceptance turned into open desire. With his silent approval, I placed my hand on her mound of black pussy hair and gently rubbed back and forth. Realizing a different presence, she opened her eyes and sat up. Seeing me she cried out. Through silent messages he eased her fears; she understood that I was to be welcomed. Their inner communications amazed me. I am sure they spoke with their minds, mind to mind. And that made me wonder how much of my thoughts they could read. I soon learned the answer. She reached out, took my hand, and placed it on her breast. Her skin was so smooth. I leaned into her and gently massaged her nipple. It was electrical.

Slowly I stroked her lovely body and played in her hair-patch.

I realized his stomach rippled and her eyes grew wide with a soft glow as he filled her with his seed. Soft sounds came from her as she climaxed. A smile of sheer delight spread across his handsome face. Then they were both still, so very still.

I rolled over onto my back, crossed my legs beneath me. My cock was very rigid and thick. They both stared at my enormity. He then took a hold of my organ and gently squeezed it, and then began to slowly pump it up and down. Her eyes grew large and filled with total admiration and desire. She disengaged herself from her lover and mounted my hot club. She struggled for a moment and then had all of me. She then assumed her former posture; leaning back until her head was on the ground. Her slit was warm and moist from his spendings. He lay beside me and began to touch me in many places, filling me with total ecstatic delight. Then he leaned down to me and kissed me.

My whole body fused. He spoke to me in whispered tones.

Bear witness to my soul.
Thou have created in me a thirst—
A thirst to know thee.
It is the power of our union
Of our bodies
Of our minds
Of our souls
That has produced this eternal marriage

48

We three are one with the Universe
I am the sun and the moon; you are the stars
Our senses rush with the waters—of the oceans,
Of the rivers and lakes.
Fly with us for we are the Whole; the eternal.

My whole being relaxed and I felt exquisite pleasure; infinite in scope, universal in its depth. Nothing has ever equaled it since.

The girl sent shock waves down my large throbbing cock; caressing it with eternal promise. The pressure built at my base and I exploded deep within her. Our seeds, his and mine, mixed at her center. She leaned over and kissed me. It was rapture personified. She removed herself from my cock and squatted beside him.

We talked about many things and I learned to listen to the earth. Above all, I learned the essence of love. Nothing in my life's journey has ever equaled that magnificent moment in time.

I learned that his name was Monte and her name was Dawn. The three of us spent the remaining of August together. Our relationship deepened and grew as our bodies, minds, and souls became one with the wind and sun. We were at peace with our Mother Earth. They were generous in providing me many hours of sexual delight.

I had convinced my parents that it was okay for me to go camping along the shores of the Big Lake. I didn't tell them about Monte or Dawn. On our second day out, Monte drew me aside.

"You have enjoyed my woman, my sex, eaten our food, and lived as one of us naked in the bosom of our Mother, the Earth. It is now time to learn the eternal secret of my people."

Monte then removed a pendant from around his neck. At first, it seemed to be a piece of clear quartz. Its moon-shape sparkled in the light of our campfire.

"Moon-shaped, you say. Describe this pendant in detail," PJ said. "Did you touch it?"

"I don't think so. Is that important?" I replied.

"It could very well be. From what you've said, your young friend was a shaman."

"A shaman?" I questioned.

"Yes. A spiritual mystic who believed in the unseen world of spirits. Shamash was the chief sun-god. Are you sure the pendant was moon-shaped?"

"It could have been. It's been a long time ago."

"Hmm," PJ said. "Continue with your story. I didn't mean to interrupt."

Monte held the pendant on its rawhide string in front of me and had me stare at its center as he slowly swung it back and forth. It was so strange. I felt myself growing as large as the Universe as I floated upward as the heavens opened before me. And all things were beautiful. My body, mind, and soul melted into one gigantic being. I encompassed all things. Then I felt his presence; his mind reached out and joined me in space. Time ceased to exist. We talked without speaking; our minds were one. He projected me further into space and showed me things I had not even imagined before. I saw vast

50

areas of snow, of a desert, high mountains, and huge jungles. And there was always the moon or sun. A face appeared—the most beautiful face imaginable. There was no body; just a divine face that smiled at me. Joy filled my heart.

"Remarkable," PJ said.

When I came back, and I have to say when I came back for I had truly been through the cosmos. I felt flush and I lay down close to Monte and wept. He placed his hand on my head and peace filled my soul. I slept.

The next morning when I woke up, Monte was sitting next to me, intensely watching me. Then he spoke to me in his own tongue.

"Ne-e-no-ll-no! You are among the perfect people."

"What do you mean," I stammered.

"Many times from now you will know. You have traveled far, my friend. You have had enough for now. Come, we will return to your parents," Monte said as he stood up.

When our stay at the lake came to an end our parting deeply saddened me. I will never forget the total loneliness I felt as I shoved off from my little island. Monet and Dawn stood there, immortal, and waved goodbye. Despite my heavy heart, I realized that what they had given me would always be a part of me; that the memory would be mine forever.

"What did you do after your return to the United States?" PJ said.

Fall was just a blimp as winter arrived all too quickly. I spent my time in training; each day I worked out in the gym and as the cold months passed I grew taller and bulked up. I enjoyed my studies. Spring arrived with a renewed anticipation as my parents again talked of our return to the lake in Canada. Unfortunately, our return brought me great grief, a sadness I still feel today.

"Sadness you still feel? Care to explain?" PJ asked.

Yes, the Indians were not there and never showed up. Monte and Dawn were not there. The Canadian Indian Agent, Marc Morand, and his family were already encamped in their summer residence. I called on Mr. Morand and asked him about my Indian friends. He could tell me nothing. He reminded me that the Montagnais were nomadic and wandered from one end of Quebec-Labrador Peninsula to the other. It seemed odd to me that Mr. Morand did not know Monte and Dawn. I thought all Natives had to be registered.

Anyway, one night, just before the high moon, I slipped out of our cabin. As I pushed my rowboat out into the water, an owl hooted. I went to my little island and to the enchanted clearing where I had spent so many happy and beautiful hours. I knelt, closed my eyes, and tried to concentrate on Monte and Dawn. I don't know why, but somehow I felt I could reach out to them wherever they were. Morning came and I was depressed. Time weighed on me and I grew more restless and depressed each passing day. I felt like I should walk out into the lake and end it all. But then reprieve came as it will do for those who wait.

"A reprieve from your suicidal thoughts," PJ asked.

"Actually boredom," I replied.

Agent Morand decided to have a party. My parents and I were invited. The invitation came at midnight from an attractive French girl. It's no small miracle that my father didn't shoot her. After hurriedly dressing, we walked the 200 yards to the Morands. When were walked in we were surprised at the number of people there. They had come up from Montreal.

Apparently, it was a custom among the traditional French-Canadians that guests were seated in straight-back chairs along the walls of the room. We were shown our place to sit by the same young girl who had come to get us. I guessed she was my age. A drink was brought to my mother and she thought she should wait for my father to be served sat there holding her drink. Everyone just continued to sit there. Mrs. Morand came to my mother and asked if there was something wrong with her drink. My mother said no that it was fine. Mrs. Morand then suggested that my mother should drink up so the rest could be served. After my mother completed her drink, my father was served. One gulp and then I was brought a drink. I looked at my parents to see what I should do. My father nodded and I down the drink. It was a rich red wine. I guessed it was homemade. The next guest was then served. Large quantities of food were brought from the kitchen; dishes and silverware were stacked on separate tables around the large room.

Then we were told to help ourselves. I only took a couple of items; nibbled at those, and then excused myself and slipped out a side door.

The French girl was sitting on the steps. She got up and started to leave. I motioned for her to stay. She told me her name was Jeanette and that she was seventeen. Her English was impeded by the obvious fact that she had been into the wine. I slipped my arm around her waist and gently pulled her to me. The light from a nearby window showed her slighted parted lips. I leaned into her and whispered, "I want to fuck you. Okay."

Jeanette didn't answer. Instead, she stood up, held out her hand, and led me away from the house. We ran along the sandy beach until we came to a small cove. She stopped giggling when I pulled her to me, sought her mouth, and began to tongue her. She caressed the back of my neck as my hands sought her supple breasts. With a gentle tug on her peasant blouse, I freed her breasts and slowly rolled each nipple until they firmed. Then I leaned down, tacking first one in my mouth and sucking it and then the other. I slowly worked my way up her smooth neck and shoulder. I felt her quiver. She suddenly pulled away from me. I thought she meant to run away. Instead stepped out of her skirt, dropped her panties, and stood before me teasing with sensual gyrations.

She lunged at me, rippling at my shirt, pulling at my belt. I had to force her hands away while I undid my belt, pants button, and dropped my shorts. She dropped to her knees and hungrily began licking my rock-hard cock. I swear I could see my cock throb as she ran her sweet tongue its full length. She moved to my large balls, struggling to get one in her mouth, and began stroking my rigid shaft up and down with one hand. I reached for her but she broke away and ran down the sandy beach. I tackled her and we fell into the lake. I placed one knee and pushed her legs apart and with the precision of a Stormtrooper, I thrust my raging cock into her willing cunt. We were so consumed with our lust for one another the waters around us churned. She grabbed my ass and pulled to get more of me into her molten slit. I felt the build-up as I exploded deep within her sweet cavern.

Then I pulled her up out of the water and carried her back onto the sandy beach. Gently, I laid her down. I stood over her, admiring her sweet newly swollen cunt. She spread her legs and I eased down on top of her and shoved my cock home. She locked her long legs around me and pushed to meet my thrusts. With a little effort and without spoiling the rhythm, Jeanette had her legs up around my neck. We created a mutual rhythmic stroke. I slowed my pace as I sucked one of her hard nipples. She thrust herself against me and I felt her shudder as she reached another orgasm.

The sun had shown itself. We slipped back into our clothes and she scurried back to the house and I headed to our cabin. I had just gotten myself to bed when my folks came in. They went to bed and I heard my mother giggle and realized they were having sex. I held a different perspective of them

55

after that. The end of August came and we headed home.

Fall came and then the winds of winter. Once again depression set itself upon me. I became restless and totally unhappy. The "kids" parties ceased to be fun or amusing. Gradually, I withdrew into my own thoughts. I refused to go places with my folks and they were forced to excuse my ill behavior as being moody because it was that 'time of seed getting.' I let them believe that. As the winter cold deepened so did my periods of depression. My desolation consumed me. Nothing seemed to fill the empty spaces of my heart.

Born out of that desperation was an avid interest in reading the great minds of the world. Dante, Bruno, Descartes, Spinoza, Leibniz, Nietzsche were just the tip of the iceberg. Plato, Socrates, and the great myths of the world filled the hours at the local library. I became such a fixture in the main reading room that the librarian no longer required me to check-in. One night she forgot I was there and had turned off the lights.

"Hey," I yelled.

"Oh, Davy, I forgot you were here," Katheryn said.

"No problem. Can I help you finish closing up?"

She turned on one set of lights and came into the small reading room where I had now sequestered myself. She was in her twenties. I know that because my mother said so. Katheryn wore her black hair in a bun and dark-rimmed glasses sat at the end of her nose.

"What are you reading now, Davy?" Katheryn said as she leaned in close to me. She smelt good and I felt gentle warmth from her. She touched my hand as she picked up a book to shelve it. I was sure her fingers lingered a bit. When she turned to the shelf her breasts touched my cheek. I slowly brought my face up.

"Here, let me help you with that," I said, lowering my voice.

As I got up from my chair and moved toward the bookshelves, I let my hand touch her on the butt. It was such a slight touch I wasn't sure she even felt it. But then I realized she stuck her butt out.

"Hmm. Nice," I whispered. "Very nice."

She turned around with such force she dropped the book she was holding. For a moment I thought she was going to hit me with it. She started to say something but didn't. I had her in my arms and began kissing her. She leaned her body into me as she whispered, "Yes, Davy."

Katheryn slipped off her shoes, dropped her skirt, and then I helped her pull off her blouse. I reached around her back, unsnapped her bra, and let it fall loose as her exquisite breasts tumbled out. With a quick movement, she lowered her shoulders and her bra fell to the floor. I began kissing each sweet nipple, bringing each to a pink firmness. She stepped back, dropped her slip as I moved my hands down her firm butt cheeks. Then I slipped one hand down the front of her white panties and began a gentle but firm rubbing between her legs. She pushed against my hand, eagerly seeking its attention. With one finger I parted her cunt lips and slowly worked my way in and then curling my finger to massage her clit. Her hot lips caressed my mouth, teasing me as she nipped my neck.

I felt her struggle with my belt, then my zipper. I sucked my gut in and my pants fell to the floor. With her fingers, she eagerly played up and down my stiff pole as it struggled to push its way over the top of my shorts. With a swift yank, she had my lusting cock free.

I slide my hands under her tight butt and pulled her up. She quickly wrapped her legs around me as I eased her down my shaft. With a quick pull, I had my cock encased and I felt her cunt muscles tighten around it. As she clung to me with her arms wrapped around my neck, she continued to kiss me and her sweet cunt massaged my cock. I couldn't get into her deep enough. She slowly pushed one of my large balls into her slit and then the second one. I shoved hard and she slammed into the bookcase. Books tumbled to the floor. I exploded.

I'm not sure what time it was when Katheryn suddenly scrambled to her feet. Her phone was ringing.

"Who? Oh my god. I bet he's still downstairs in the reading room. I don't remember him saying good night when I closed the library. Hang on and I'll go see. No, it's no problem. I can certainly understand your concern that he's not home at this late hour."

58

She placed a finger on my lips and whispered that it was my mother.

"Mrs. Fuchs, yes he's here. He's sound asleep. I'll wake him up and send him along home. Goodness, I'm embarrassed because I didn't double-check that everyone had left the library. I certainly will from now own."

I got up, dressed, puller her to me for one more kiss and a feel of her still wet crotch. On my way home I thought there certainly was some truth about having an older woman. Jeanette was seventeen but Katheryn was twenty-two and she was totally awesome.

Two months later Katheryn suddenly resigned as the librarian. My mother told me Katheryn's mother was very ill and she had to go and take care of her. I thought that was strange since I was sure Katheryn had said her mother had passed away the year before she took the job as librarian.

"So, you think you impregnated her?" PJ asked.

"All I can say, that a couple of the high school girls had to leave town to take care of an ill aunt and it was rumored that they were pregnant."

"Hmm. It's time for breakfast. PJ said.

"If you don't mind I'd like to skip breakfast. I need to get out. Maybe walk along the lake. Get some fresh air."

"Of course, no problem. You can have something when you get back."

"Why don't you come with me? It's a beautiful morning," I said.

PART TWO

Our walk was slow because of PJ's need to use a cane. We ended up sitting on a bench in the park near his home. He urged me to go on ahead which I did. I couldn't help but wonder if all this "confession" was doing me any good. Every time I related any details about one of my sexual encounters the urge to fuck came back. And wasn't one of the purposes of these sessions to eventually control this unquenchable urge to have sex. Restless is an understatement. I began to run and I soon passed PJ dozing in the warm sun. I ran the walkway once more and stopped at the bench.

"Ah, so you have gotten rid of some of your tension. Good. Do you think you could have some breakfast now? I'm starving," PJ said as he eased himself up.

He shook himself, stomped each foot, and took me by the arm and we headed back to his house. Much to my surprise breakfast was served by a very attractive redhead. From her build and looks I guessed she was in her early twenties. She had a nice ass.

PJ noticed my admiring looks.

"Her name is Sarah Jane. She fills in when Joseph has the weekend off.

Once Sarah Jane had cleared the table and left, PJ said, "I remember in one of the letters you mentioned you had given in to a desire for private revenge. I would very much like to hear about that, but right now I have some news for you."

"News?" I said.

"Yes, I have called an old friend in the Canadian Department of Indian Affairs. He has agreed to try and track down your two Indian friends," PJ said.

"Man, that would be great."

"What were their names; Indian and Christian names?"

"His name Night Bird and Monte; hers is Dawn. I think her Indian name is Bird Song or Singing-Bird."

"That will have to do. I know how much they meant to you but don't get your hopes up. My friend may not be able to find anything. I know you have been disappointed and taken advantage of during your search for them. I am going north and I will be gone at least three days."

"North? You mean back to the Lake? Can I go with you?"

"Yes and no. You shouldn't go. I understand that there has been some trouble there among the Montagnais and an outsider might not be welcome." PJ said.

"Oh, but it's okay for you to go."

"At this point, yes it is. I have worked with several of the tribal members and have a fairly good relationship with them."

"Do you know what kind of trouble? I don't want you placing your life in danger because of me."

"From what I have learned there have been some strange deaths; suicides I'm told. I do not feel there is any danger to me. If I find out anything about your two friends I will immediately let you know."

"It still worries me," I replied.

"While I am away, the place is yours. Amuse yourself in any way that best suits you. The staff will see to your needs. I'm having a car brought around to drive me to the lake," PJ said.

"So who is driving you? I don't see what that couldn't be me," I said still not happy about being left behind.

"The son of one of the Montagnais leaders. He was one of my students at the University. I won't leave for a couple of hours. He has classes until 2:30 and it will take him at least an hour to get here. We have time if you want to talk about your desire for revenge on the Kahlil girls."

"Okay. At fifteen I stood at six feet and weighed in at 160 pounds. I was very blonde as I am now. My mother said my blue eyes deepened. Unlike many of my contemporaries, I was not cursed with acne. My cock was a full eight inches in length. Relatives said I was good looking; family friends who had daughters said I was handsome. The girls at schools called me 'dream-boat', a disgusting name while the guys openly envied my build."

"I was so indebted to Monte and Dawn for teaching me the ways of self-fulfillment simply because it allowed me to keep a level head during all that praise. I'm sure it would have gone to my head. Don't misunderstand, I was and still am proud of my body."

"Spring's warmth was most welcome to me. My soul came alive. My parents sold their holdings in the Valley and had given over to town life. Old Valley friends fell by the wayside or just generally forgotten. However, this particular spring my parents decided to return to the Valley to see the Kahlils. Mr. Kahlil and my father spent the day fishing. The women-folk as they were referred to by their husbands spent their time talking and baking. I spent most of my time outdoors soaking up the warm spring sun. It seemed to me that even the very bones of my body were cold from a long harsh winter.

After dinner, the Kahlils and my parents went up the road to the old hotel for dancing and drinks. The two Kahlil girls and I were left at home. Small talk during a board game ended when they went to bed. I noticed Donna, the eighteen-year-old, and the younger of the two girls always managed to touch my hand or bumped my knee. I waited for a time and then quietly climbed the stairs to the bedrooms. The light from the hallway was enough for me to see that Donna was naked. I eased into her room, dropped my clothes, and set my throbbing cock free. She sensed my presence and opened her eyes. Before she could speak, I bent down and kissed her as I rubbed her sweet soft fury patch.

Donna wrapped her arms around my neck and whispered, "Yes" as she eagerly pushed against my

"Oh my god. You are not a little boy anymore. You're a naughty boy," Bev giggled as she leaned up to kiss me.

I rolled over on top of her, aimed my throbbing cock, and shoved. It went into its hilt. I felt my balls dangle along her open cunt. I felt her hands grab my ass. She pulled me in deeper into her pulsing clit. It was obvious she was not a virgin by the way she massaged my cock. She brought a new meaning to pleasure. She bucked beneath me, groaning.

"Shoot it to me, Davy. Shoot it to me," Bev moaned.

She heaved up with my downward thrust. The bed rocked so hard it banged against the wall. I was sure Donna had to have heard. I felt the river pressure me, building, rushing to explode. I was pumping her like crazy. She had her legs wrapped around me as well as her arms. She gasped and lay very still. My juice flew out of me. I thought I had killed her. I was mistaken. As I eased my still hard cock from her very wet mons, she slid down between my legs and began to massage my glans. First the bottom of my cock's head; then around each side, her sweet tongue flew. Then she tongued my entire shaft, pulling first one of my large balls into her mouth and then the other. I felt the urge build and my buttocks contracted. She swallowed and had my cock down her throat. My juice flew out. She gurgled just once. I felt her tongue lick my still engorged dick. With forced suction, she drained my cock as she removed her lips.

I got up, went back to my room. I humped my pillow and waited for dawn to break."

"How did you feel after that?" PJ asked.

"Honestly, I felt pretty damn good. Almost like my old self," I said.

"And that ended your revenge on the Kahlil girls?" PJ said.

"Not quite. After a breakfast of ham, eggs, and griddle cakes I suggested going for a ride along the 'switchbacks,' a long narrow and steep road up a local mountain. The road was built by loggers back in the day. You drove up one incline, backed up to make the turn to head up the next incline. I thought it would be cool to stop at our old schoolhouse. Bev was readily agreeable, but Donna had to be urged by her parents to go. I'm sure Bev would have been happy to leave Donna behind.

We stopped at our old schoolhouse first. It was empty and deserted. Students were now bussed into town. We got out walked around. We joked about some of the things each of us used to do and how we made fun of the teacher. We piled back into Bev's Chevy and headed for the switchbacks. I sat in the middle. Bev was driving. As we eased our way around one of the many sharp curves I leaned into Donna and squeezed her tit. She yelped.

"What's the matter?" Donna asked.

"I just squeezed her tit," I said. Turning to Donna, I continued, "It's okay. I screwed Bev last night, also. She liked it just like you did."

"I'll be damned," Bev exclaimed.

66

"You should be, greedy," I laughed.

With that introduction of the truth, I yanked up their dresses and exposed their completely naked pussies. I immediately busied my hands in their fur patches. Both giggled. Donna was hot almost immediately.

"Drive around nice and slow. I am going to give Donna another good fucking," I said.

Donna was rubbing my already hard cock as I said, "Easy girl. Unzip my pants and let me out. I pushed my pants down as I kicked off my shoes.

"Mount that hot cock, Donna," I said as she pulled her dress up over her head and finally off giving me access to her sweet tits. I nipped each one.

She came down on my huge cock and because she was already moist I went all the way in. I put my hand on her naked butt and helped her go up and down my throbbing shaft. She hit her peak and went into another orgasm. She groaned loudly as she sought my pleasure stick. Bev it a bump in the dirt road and I'm sure one of my balls went into Donnas dripping wet cunt. Donna was wild as I shot a hot load into her burning clit. I reached over, turned off the ignition and the car glided to a smooth halt.

"Your turn, Bev. Meet me in the back seat. More room," I said as I lifted Donna off of me.

I didn't have to say anymore. She had her clothes off and in the back seat before I was.

Hurry, Davy. Shove it to me," Bev moaned as I slid my engorged cock into her already moist clit.

Within a few short minutes, she came. I continued to ream her swollen cunt until I shot my wad.

"My god, Davy, that was even better than last night," Bev said as Donna climbed into the back of the car with us.

"My pleasure," I said as I drawled out the word ma'am."

Donna began licking my cock. And then Bev joined her. Greedily, they sucked me. I popped another load, but I'm not sure which one took it. We climbed back into the front seat and headed to the farm. I remained naked so they could play with me until just before Bev drove us into the driveway. My family and I left that evening."

"Did you see the girls again?" PJ asked.

"No. Well, that's not true. I saw them when they and their parents came to my father's funeral. That was four years later. I had heard Donna had been pregnant but no one mentioned anything about her having a kid.

That orgy, and that's what it was, with the Kahlil girls snapped me out of my depressed existence. I felt renewed. My confidence returned. I was able to focus on all that I had read, learned, and done. Out of that came a new and very personal belief, one which I follow today. Monte and Dawn must be given credit for its beginning and that is why I want to find them. Some gaps need to be filled in."

"So, when you went to Canada that summer, your . . ."

"I didn't go. Instead, I enrolled in summer school," I interrupted PJ. "I took French and Latin. My teacher, Miss Ginger Brecht turned out to be an excellent teacher in more ways than in just French and Latin."

"And how was that?" PJ asked.

"Miss Brecht was a petite attractive woman with long black hair and dark brown eyes that glistened. Of course, I noted her breasts. They were not large but big enough for her small body. She wore tight-fitting blouses which seemed to make her tits look bigger. Sometimes she wore very tight skirts that emphasized her tight ass. One day, however, she wore a flowing red skirt and a white top that had a plunging neckline. I sat in the front row along the classroom windows and could see she wasn't wearing a bra. She sat on the edge of her desk, facing the class. She caught me not paying attention.

"Davy, stop staring out the window. Move to the other side of the room, and pay attention," Miss Brecht scolded.

"But I like the view where I'm at," I shot back.

She swiveled around on her desk as she said, "The view is eyes forward. Now move it."

I should have noticed before. As I changed seats I saw she had no panties on. I said, "Yes, ma'am. Eyes forward."

I gave her my best smile. She smiled back as she said, "You're very bright, Davy, but you do need to pay attention.

"Yes, ma'am. I do pay attention most of the time, but you lost me on that neuter stuff. Would you mind helping me with that?"

"Of course."

I just wanted to hang around. I guess I was feeling a bit lonely with my parents gone. I was feeling horny. After a half-hour session, I left and went out to the parking lot to wait for her. Within a few minutes, she walked into the parking lot.

"Miss Brecht, I missed my ride. Do you mind giving me a lift?"

"No problem, Davy. Be glad to."

I piled into her Chevy, settled my ass in the seat, and spread my legs wide apart. My left leg rested against her. She didn't attempt to move it away. I began talking.

"My parents won't be back until the end of next week."

"Oh, I didn't know your parents were away," Miss Brecht said.

"Yeah, they are back in Canada."

"Why didn't you go with them?"

"Couple of reasons. The most important was I wanted to take French," replied.

She caught my smile and replied, "I just bet you did." She laughed.

I liked her laugh. It was natural and easy.

"I have to stop at the store. Do you mind waiting?"

"Heck, no. Beggars can't be choosers," I said as I got out of the car, walked around to her side, and opened the door. She was impressed. She wasn't

70

gone long. I helped her load her groceries into the back of the car. As she pulled into our long driveway she said, "I've been thinking, Davy. Maybe you might like to come over to my apartment for dinner. You might enjoy a home-cooked meal. Your folks being away."

"Better idea. I have a large steak out of the freezer. More than I can eat. Why not come on it and eat here?" I said as casual as I could.

"Well, I suppose it would be alright," she said with a touch of hesitation in her voice.

"Of course it's alright, Miss Brecht. My folks won't mind," I replied playing dumb at her implication of concern.

"Would you like a drink, Miss Brecht?" I said as I pushed a button and a panel on the wall opened to reveal a well-stocked bar.

"I'm not sure I should," she replied.

"It's okay. Besides this is my home and who is going to ever know that you had a before-dinner cocktail, "I said as I began to make two martinis.

"Well, I suppose it's alright. Just one and do you think you should?"

"Sure, my folks offered me a drink before dinner and there's always just the right wine with dinner. Speaking of, I have a great red wine to go with our steaks."

I made a pitcher of martinis and they were five to one. I figured it would help her relax. I poured her drink and handed it to her and then poured one for me and joined her on the couch. I reached over in front of us to a coffee table and opened a silver box, and offered her a cigarette. I took one, lit it, and took a slow drag, and then offered it to her.

"You are a perfect host, Davy," she said as she kicked her shoes off and curled her legs up on the couch.

"Nice company," I replied.

"This is an excellent martini. Total perfection," she said.

"It's all a part of the family tradition," I replied as I refilled her glass.

Pretending to fill my glass, I sat the crystal pitcher back on the bar. I sat down beside her as she slowly nursed her drink. I stretched my legs out in front of me and let my manliness show as my pants tightened over its growing size. She leaned back, kicked off her shoes, and curled her shapely legs under her, and turned to face me.

"That's a nice perfume you're wearing. What is it called?" I said as I spread my legs a bit more.

"Thank you. It's Fleur de Tempt. I bought it in Paris last summer. You, Davy, are a very observant person," she said patting my outstretched leg.

I leaned forward, sniffed the back of her neck. As I did I bumped her hand and the martini spilled down the front of her dress. I immediately began brushing the front of her dress. Her breasts were small but firm. I grabbed a couple of napkins and continued to wipe the front of her dress. She was all apologies and embarrassed. I was embarrassed for her and that when I took her in my arms and kissed her. At first, she resisted, and then as I sought her tongue she yielded and returned my kiss. I held

72

her tightly as my tongue darted in and out of her sweet mouth. I caught her tongue and held it. She pushed back gasping. I thought she was going to cry.

"I'm sorry." I said, "I shouldn't have done that. Forgive me."

"It's okay, Davy. It just never happened."

"How about those steaks? I'm really hungry," I said.

"Me, too," she replied as she smiled.

I smiled back. When I got up she could easily see I was hungry for more than a steak. My pistol was cocked.

"Hey, we better get you some dry clothes," I said. "Come with me."

I noticed her looking at my fly. I shoved my hips forward to tighten my pants.

"Follow me," I said.

I led her upstairs to my bedroom where I fished around for a pair of my pajamas and a robe. I handed them to her and started to leave.

"I'm sorry to be such a bother, Davy. Really, I am."

"You're no bother. None at all." I lied. She was bothering a part of me big time.

"Before you leave, would you unhook my dress? My hair is caught in the snap."

I unsnapped her dress and it slipped down over her shoulders as she leaned forward. I pulled her to me, wrapped one leg around her small body, and pressed my throbbing cock against her. I sought her sweet mouth, found it, and kissed her. I undid her bra and let it tumble away. Her breasts were milk-white and their nipples were pink. I bent down to them, kissed each, sucking ever so gently on each sweet nub until it firmed.

"Oh, Davy, Davy," She whispered.

I pulled her dress down and then her slip. I eased my right hand inside her panties and began to gently rub her already firm mons. I felt her quiver as I slide my middle finger into her moist cunt. She had her arms around my neck, kissing me as she wrapped one leg around me, giving me greater access to her hot pussy. With a quick pull, I had her panties off. I tongued her from her tits to her sweet moist clit. She gasped as I began to explore her sweetness with my tongue.

I gently laid her down on my bed. I removed her stockings and shoes and then removed my shirt and pants. As I dropped my shorts, I let my huge throbbing cock bob up and down, she reached out and gently massaged my large balls and slowly worked her fingers to the top of my glans.

"Nice, huh?" I said smiling at her.

I lowered myself down on her as my cock eased its way into her willing crack. I slid my hands under buttocks and pulled her to me as my engorged cock made itself at home. I gently kissed her; caressing her mouth with my tongue. She nipped at my earlobe as I pulled my cock back and then slammed it to her.

"Oh, Davy, I'm so hungry. Feed me, every wonderful inch," Ginger whispered.

"Don't worry about that. I'll feed you plenty."

And feed her I did. There was no letup in my reaming her very wet canal. Drenched with sweat, I finally exploded, filling her with my hot cum. She swooned. That scared me. I'd never had anyone do that before. Frantically, I began rubbing her hands, feet, legs. She opened her eyes and I breathed a sigh of relief.

"I'm alright, Davy," Ginger said as she wrapped her arms around me.

As I got up, I handed her a robe. We went downstairs and prepared our dinner. While she cooked, I made a game of feeling her up and she grabbing my cock. The steaks were great. I opened a bottle of chilled wine and filled two glasses.

"I better get dressed and leave," she said as we stacked the dishes.

"Not yet," I replied as I pressed my rigid cock against her.

I sat down on a chair and she mounted my rock hard cock. She rode me fast and furious. Her firm breast bounced up and down as she continued her onslaught of my happy dick. We came together that time. I tried to get her to stay the night but she wasn't having it. I hit the bed as soon as she left. I slept so soundly I was nearly late for school. In class, no one would have ever guessed what had transpired between us.

Ginger stopped me after class and said, "Dinner at my place?"

"What time?" I replied.

"Why not come over now? Give me a few minutes to get things organized for tomorrow's class."

We spent the afternoon and on into the night in total sexual rapture. There seemed to be no end to her thirst for my willing cock.

I hated to see the summer end. Our last time together was in our local park. It was even better, if that was possible, under the stars. She dropped me off at my house just as the sun broke. I was quite sure I was madly in love.

Unfortunately, when school opened Ginger was not there. A man now offered the second course in French. Class was not the same and I didn't have a great deal of enthusiasm. Fall drifted into early winter. One night my father called me into his office.

"Now, Davy, I want some straight answers. You know I don't cotton much to a lot of the gossip spread by old women, but it seems there is considerable truth to what is being said. Straight answers, no mind you."

"Yes. Of course," I replied.

"Have you lived with that French teacher last summer while your mother and I were away?"

"Sir?"

"Have you been screwing that teacher?"

"I-I. Yes, damn it. I have. And I know what people have said about her. She is not a whore."

"Now don't go flying off the handle. Nobody here called her a whore. This is a serious thing, Davy. I only hope you realize the seriousness of the

76

consequences. I certainly can understand a young man being enamored by the attentions of an older woman, especially an attractive one."

"She didn't lead me astray. I started the affair. I admit I sort of went a little wild.

"Well, it's over. You understand? She's moved on and you need to do the same. According to Doc Jones, she left because she's pregnant."

"My—mine?" I whispered.

"Could be unless you protected yourself."

"No. If she's pregnant it's because I knocked her up."

I felt sick on my stomach and at the same time, I fought back the urge to cry.

"I've ruined her life. Shit. I need to—."

"It's been taken care of. You better go to bed. School tomorrow. And Davy, chalk this up as one of life's experiences and next time don't be so careless. You understand?"

I nodded my head, turned, and went to my room. I felt miserable. And then the joy of the summer filled me. And it was good. Certainly what was so good couldn't be all bad. I heard them talking. My father was explaining to my mother that every young man had to sow his wild oats. I detected a bit of pride in his voice. I think he was pleased to learn his son was a man to his way of thinking.

Unfortunately, it was after that I experienced severe depression. My parents kept such a tight rein on me I was seldom ever out of their sight if I wasn't in school. Pills were prescribed by the first psychiatrist. That didn't work. I just fidgeted. The second psychiatrist wasn't any better and the third tried to get me to have sex with him. I wrote to you all the gory details.

"Yes, I still have your letters. I thought you might want them someday. I had to admit, Davy, you took me on a merry chase with your probing questions," P.J. said.

"One of the many reasons for my many letters was your recognition as one of the world's leading anthroposophists and your wide knowledge of the Canadian Indian," I said.

"Thank you for your kind compliments. I'm just an idle meddler in the nature of man," P.J. said as a smile formed along his lips.

"And a very capable one at that," I replied.

CHAPTER THREE

"So, according to your letters, you believe man is begotten of the cosmos," P.J. said.

"Yes, I do. And I believe there is an organic living interaction between all parts of that universe. Furthermore, because of that interaction, man cannot be discounted. It is only through the unity of the body, mind, and soul that we comprehend the ultimate construct of our world."

"Ah, I see from your perspective man is still climbing after that ineffable knowledge, infinite and always changing?" P.J. said.

"Of course, Doc. Even during my own time of despair I understood that like the restless winds, I was working myself to reach the ripest fruit of all— perfect bliss; that suit fruition of eternal universality I call fecundity."

"Hmm, then you are suggesting a finite intellect cannot employing comparison, reach the ultimate truth."

"Correct. Only as man seeks the infinite can he see that truth that can be the only exact measure of truth," I said nodding my head.

"What I hear you saying is that when and that is the operative word, man transcends to the level of universality, he is himself, truth," P.J. said.

"Da Vinci touched on this when he said that a 'lover is drawn to the thing loved; and that the sense is by that which it perceives, and unites with it, they become one and the same thing.'"

"Thus rejoicing, pleasure, and satisfaction," P.J. replied.

"Thus, fecundity," I replied.

"Hmm, do you also accept the tenet that images or objects are spread throughout the air which surrounds them?" P.J. questioned.

"Especially so after my experiences at the lake with Monte. All objects are in every point the same."

"I see. Then you accept the idea that the images of our spheres enter and past together will all other bodies through a natural point in which merge and become united—a whole," P.J. said.

"Universality! And remember, man is an equal force inside nature and the same through time," I replied.

"That is when he is one with himself," P.J. said as a broad smile parted his lips.

"Exactly, and that is what my long search has been all about—to become one with myself. To arrive at fecundity."

"Remarkable. I would very much like to discuss this further with you but there are preparations I have to make before making the trip north so my friend, you must excuse me," P.J. said as he slowly eased himself up from his chair. "I have an early start tomorrow. Good night."

"Be sure to wake me," I said.

Sleep was fitful. I kept having dreams. Dreams? I should say videos for they were far more than just fleeting images; they lasted and the voices were very clear. I tried to relax so my mind could reach out. I couldn't. Meditation irritated me. I became distressed and that destroyed the mind-videos.

A young maid came to my room and woke me. I had not seen her before. When I questioned P.J. he said she was a temporary replacement for his aide who would be driving him north.

"She's a very attractive young woman," I said as I sipped my coffee.

"Yes, I agree with you. Perhaps she will help you pass the time while I am away."

I felt a slight flush on my face.

P.J. left immediately after our early breakfast and I was left to wander around in his huge old house. There were at least a dozen rooms I had not seen. I assumed the remaining rooms would be at least the same size as those I had seen. There were three *sitting rooms*, a music room, six bedrooms, a huge professional kitchen, a ballroom, and an office, and two bathrooms; one joined his office, the other a part of my bedroom. There were servant quarters which included a small kitchen, three bedrooms, and a sitting room. I assumed the bedrooms besides mine each had their bathroom. I counted 8 fireplaces and three balconies. Every room was richly furnished; beautiful old tapestries, paintings by some of the great artists, and sculptures were appropriately placed throughout the mansion. It was a museum.

There is no question about it; P.J. is a very wealthy man. I thought my father had left me well off and even with my successful investments, I was poor by comparison. I enjoyed poking around and being by myself for a while. Time quietly slipped away. After a lunch of seafood and vintage wine, I returned to my rooms for the rest of the afternoon. There I began to read one of the several books P.J. had left for me, all dealt with metaphysics. I almost didn't hear the tapping at my door. It was the new maid. Her smell was intoxicating. I remembered P.J. had said her name was Merida.

"Dinner is ready, sir," she said.

"It's Merida, isn't it?"

"Yes," she said with a smile.

"I wonder if you and Joseph would join me. I hate eating alone since I've had the pleasure of P.J.'s company. I can come to the kitchen. I noted there was a place there to eat."

"I'll ask Joseph. I am sure he'd enjoy some company. I know I would," Merida said as she turned to walk away. She stopped, looked back over her shoulder, smiled, and said, "Thank you."

Dinner was going to be a pleasure. I couldn't help but notice the pointed nipples showing beneath her white blouse. Within minutes my phone rang. It was Merida. Dinner was ready to be served. She wanted to know what wine I wanted. I told her to pick one she liked.

We chatted along as we ate, enjoying the wine, and friendship. Merida slipped her hand beneath the table and began to gently rub my leg. I greeted her hand with mine and led it to my erect crotch. Her gentle rub became a stroke as she ran her fingers along the top of my thick cock. Desert was served

82

with coffee. After that, I suggested we journey to the upper deck and enjoy a sherry. Joseph declined. Merida said, "I'd love to. Just let me help Joseph clean up. Is there a particular sherry you prefer?"

"Alvear or Osborne would be nice," I replied. "See you shortly. And Joseph, you outdid yourself. The food was great."

Merida arrived with Alvear and another delight: She was naked. My pole stood at immediate attention, thickened, and pushed against my paints. With a quick shove, I had my pants and shorts off and with a swift kick, they flew across the floor. She sat the glasses of sherry down, kneeled, and began licking my rigid cock. With expert care, she curled her sweet tongue around my wide glans and guided it down the full length of my throbbing shaft until she came to my big balls. She licked first one then the other and then took each into her mouth.

"Enough! Mount me," I moaned.

I grabbed her tight ass, lifted her up, and as she spread her legs, I rammed my cock home. Eagerly, I sought her sweet nipples as she raced up and down my throbbing shaft. She groaned as she peaked. Her whole body shook as her orgasm exploded I poured a river of hot juice into her. Gently, I eased her limp body off my still engorged cock; picked her up, and went to my rooms.

I removed the rest of her clothes, stripped my clothes off, I spread her legs, and sought her hot cunt with my tongue. I felt her shudder as she pushed upward to take more of my tongue. I rose from her, and with one shove my cock again filled her sweet cunt. I stayed that way; not moving, just letting her pulsing bring me off.

I woke up to the smell of fresh coffee. She was gone. I showered and went down to breakfast. As she placed the warmed plate of Canadian bacon and eggs in front of me, she leaned forward and kissed me.

"I have the day off if you're ..."

I moved the plate of food to one side, picked her up, and set her on the table. She leaned back, spreading her legs. She had no panties on, and once again she offered me her still swollen cunt. The table moaned under the force of my thrusts. Each time she met me with an eager thrust of her own.

I removed myself; she slid off the table, straightened her skirt, and then said, "Race you back to your rooms."

I grabbed a couple of slices of Canadian bacon and followed her. Breakfast will never be the same again. She remained in my bed fucking me. No woman had consumed me the way she had. The fourth day brought P.J. back.

I'm not sure who was more surprised him or me. P.J. was pensive and his eyes showed his consternation. He seemed old and worn. By the way, he looked at me I guess he felt the same about me. I must have shown my exhaustion from the frenzied sex for the last three days.

"Well, Davy shall we go into the library and I will tell you what I have learned?" P.J. said as he heaved a sigh.

"You are very tired. Let's wait until tomorrow morning. After breakfast, perhaps?

"Thank you. I would like that. By the way, Davy, I take it you enjoyed your time while I was away," P.J. smiled.

"Yes, very much and thank you for making sure I was taken care of."

P.J. went to his private chambers. I went to the library; there I picked up a copy of Bentham's Philosophy of Hedonism. "Funny, how some people view my basic tenets as hedonistic. Probably because of my emphasis on fulfilling one's sexual needs. What these critics don't get is that my position is that the body cannot be separated from the mind and the soul. All three need to be considered from a unification point of view. And, I might add, all three need to be cultivated to their highest form of actualization."

I suddenly realized I was talking out loud. I sat down in one of the large leather chairs to read. It wasn't long before my eyelids drooped and I gave in to sleep. Suddenly, I felt the presence of someone in the room. I sat straight up, intense, and afraid. I heard my heart beating.

"Who's there?" I said barely above a whisper.

Monte came through the window and stood before me, naked to his waist, he wore the white medallion around his neck. It glowed against his tan chest. I reached out to touch him. My hand passed through the air. I realized I was experiencing a macrophysical phenomenon. Somehow for some reason, Monte was trying to reach me; trying to tell me something. I strained to make him understand I was tuned in to his thought waves. His image blurred. Forcing myself to concentrate, his image came back and was vividly clear.

Blood was splashing down his chest. He was so pale.

"Davy, Davy, beware."

"Beware? Beware of what?" I whispered.

"Beware of the dawn. Death waits."

"I don't understand. Explain!" I felt the panic tighten its grip around my heart.

"Beware, Davy."

I felt a rush of air. He was gone. I was shaking. Desperately, I tried to regain my self-control. Perspiration made my hair matt and my breathing was difficult. I felt the blood rush to my head. I slumped into a chair and managed to push a call button on a table. Joseph rushed into the library. He must have thought something had happened to P.J. because he hadn't taken the time to put his clothes on. His nakedness was a shock and brought me to my senses. I realized I was still pushing the button.

"Joseph," I gasped. "I need Dr. Saulo."

He left and with a few minutes, I was aware of the light tread of slippered feet hurrying along the hallway to the library. I tried to get up from the chair but could not. J.P. with a look of alarm, said, "Good God, man what is wrong?"

I again tried to get up but could not. I tried to focus. P.J. looked so strange with his white hair askew and his robe hanging half off his shoulders and being held in place by a tight sash.

"You look like you've seen a ghost," P.J. said.

"I have. Monte was just here and it was a terrible experience."

"That's not possible; he's dead."

"I figured he was since you didn't tell me as soon as you returned. And then there was the blood."

"Blood? Where?"

"It was flowing out of his chest, I replied.

"Then it must have been Monte," P.J. said.

"How is that?"

"Monte was killed by a stab to the chest. According to the police, it was self-inflicted."

"I don't believe that. He simply would not have committed suicide. When and where did this happen?" I stammered.

"It happened on the old reservation. About a week ago."

"What about Dawn?" I asked.

"She is there but she wouldn't see me or talk to me. Strange since she knew I was there representing you," J.P. said.

"I just don't understand. Maybe Monte was trying to warn me about her," I said.

"Warn you?"

"Yes, Monte said, 'Beware of the dawn. Death waits.' And he repeated the warning. He must have meant Dawn, not the dawn," I said. "More likely I misheard because I was so shaken up."

"Possibly. Be cautious. I brought back something for you," P.J. said as he reached into a pocket of his robe.

He handed me a small birch bark box tied with rawhide and an envelope. I quickly tore open the envelope. It was a letter and as I read it, its magnitude rushed over me and I began to cry. Tears rushed down my face as a desperate sob escaped my open mouth. With trembling hands, I handed the letter to P.J.

Davy,

Since you are reading this I am no more.
    Many times I have been at your side, yet you did not recognize me. You are
forgiven because the truth had not come to you. It is time for you to know   that truth.

    My time with you is over. If I could change that I would. It is not to be.

    My grandfather, He-Who-Knows-All, passed to me a sacred amulet as did his father's father before him. It is now my turn. Since there will be no son to
    follow after me, I am denied my link to that which is eternal,—a choice that was not mine to make. I had hoped that our seed would have mixed and Dawn would have given up a son. That was not to be. That which has come to me is from the stars and it cannot be denied. What is, is and what will be, will be.

88

The face you saw when we were together on our little island was your own and as the river of rivers flow into one and the moon of moons blinks in unison, our destiny was sealed.

I have instructed Dr. Saulo to give you this most sacred of all things sacred.
It sources all that is past and all that is future. Wear it close to your heart and let its beat join that of your heart.

I will come to you once more. Look for me as we pass through time.

Monte

I had some difficulty getting the rawhide undone so I could open the small white birch bark box. Once open, it revealed a black stone medallion with what appeared to be an uncut diamond in its center. It was attached to a string of black beads. As I began to remove it, P.J. grabbed my hand and pushed it away.

"Don't touch it. It's as I suspected. Monte was the Shaman of the Montagnais. That medallion is the sacred authority of the most powerful shaman of all Native healers."

"But Monte said it had been passed down from the grandfathers. Why would he give me something that would be harmful?' I protested.

89

"Perhaps even on your little island, he was practicing his new powers on you. And even now, in death, he has reached out to you," P.J. replied.

"You sound as if you believe this stone is evil."

"Perhaps it is. Many rumors have floated out of the mountains of the North."

"What kind of rumors?" I said.

"The Magic One and that is what he who held the medallion was called, was greatly feared. His fame reached to Vancouver and I am told he was even known in your country. Those who crossed him suddenly disappeared," P.J. continued.

"Why would Monte wish to harm me? We are friends—rather were—friends."

"He didn't and that was because he most likely believed you were the one long told about in Native lore. And as he was commanded, he gave you his wife, and now how his sacred authority. You have been chosen as the new shaman."

"How can that be? I'm not a Native. Man, this is so damn confusing."

"Not really. Perhaps we now have the answer why Dawn would not see me," P.J. replied.

"Explain," I said.

"If she believed you to be the new shaman she most likely believed you knew all and would know she had murdered Monte. Stands to reason, don't you agree?" P.J. said as he heaved a sigh.

"Incredible. But you are right."

"There is one other thing. My research revealed a legend among the Natives that said whoever held the amulet would receive the key to a fabulous fortune. If this is indeed true, then Dawn had a motivation to kill Monte. What she didn't know is that Monte had already transferred the crystal to you."

"But, how did you get it?" I asked.

"His lawyer in Maniwaki gave it to me."

"This is so unreal. So much has happened," I said as I slouched down in a chair.

"There's no reason for me to go back to bed. Let's have something to eat and we can continue your story if you are up to it," P.J. said.

Joseph soon arrived with a tray of food and hot tea. After we had finished off the food I felt comfortable enough to put the Monte issue behind me and to continue with my story.

CHAPTER FOUR

At seventeen I was given a new convertible for my graduation from high school. I took a solo trip back to the Reservation in Canada to see if I could find Monte and Dawn. I had no luck. They had just disappeared. Anyway, that fall I entered college, one of the Eastern schools. I had signed up for the Liberal Arts. There certainly wasn't a whole lot of liberality when it came to the choices I had open to me. To take an introductory course in philosophy I had to make a big issue out of it. Evidently, one did not take philosophy as a first-semester freshman.

After a month I wasn't sure college was for me. I began to lose weight. It wasn't that I wasn't eating. The dorms were so noisy all night long I couldn't sleep. It wasn't until around four in the morning that I could get in any studying so I walked around in a sleepy stupor much of the time. I began going to the student union to study. Believe it or not, it was a lot quieter than the dorms. One afternoon while I was at the union I met Louise, the manager. I had seen her around several times and thought she was an attractive woman in her late twenties or early thirties. I also noticed she didn't pay particular attention to the students.

I was in my usual corner by a window deeply involved in my philosophy assignment when she walked over and sat down at my table. She had her blond hair in a flip which gave her a sassy look. Her tight blouse accentuated firm breasts.

"You're Davy, aren't you?" She asked.

"Yes, Davy Niles," I replied looking up from my book.

"I'm Louise Anderson. I've noticed you spend a lot of time here and always with your nose stuck in a book," she said.

"It's quieter in here than in the dorms. I can't sleep or study there. So many of the guys spend their time running around, yelling, and playing loud music," I replied

"Oh, you'll get used to it. Everyone does," Louise said as her smile exploded across her lips.

I noticed how perfectly formed they were.

"I don't think so. I'm looking for a place of my own or at least a room," I replied as I shifted my eyes to her breasts.

"Apartments are hard to come by," she said

"Tell me about it. I've been all over the area. The upperclassmen seem to have the market cornered. I looked at a couple yesterday but they weren't fit for a pig to live in let alone a human being. Nothing in this morning's paper except a couple on the other side of the campus."

"Have you tried finding a room? Some places even have kitchen privileges," Louise said.

"No, but I'm sure something will eventually turn up."

"I'm sure it will. Would you like a refill on your coffee? Maybe even a fresh cup?"

"That would be great," I said as I shoved a buck across the table.

As she crossed the large open room I watched the gentle sway of her hips. She had good legs. She was back with a full pot of coffee and two clean cups before I had finished reading the next section. She poured the coffee and sat down. She didn't say anything so I went back to my reading.

"Davy, I was thinking I have a big house with several large rooms. Maybe you'd like to——."

"Maybe your husband wouldn't like having another man in the house. I know I wouldn't," I interrupted.

"I'm a widow, going on two years," she said just above a whisper.

"Sorry to hear that. I might take you up on your offer," replied.

"It would be quiet and you could eat in. That is if you wanted to. I'll tell you what. Why not come over this afternoon to see if you'd like the place. If you do, we can discuss arrangements."

Her smile was most inviting so I agreed.

"How about an address?"

"Better yet, stick around for another hour and you can ride with me."

"Great if you don't mind bringing me back to the dorms," I said smiling back at her.

Louise slide out from behind the table and started to leave; stopped, and turned back toward me.

"It would be nice to have a man around the once," she said as leaned forward just enough to show more cleavage.

I tried to go back to my studies but that was a useless endeavor. My mind kept mulling over the possibilities, all kinds of very interesting possibilities that could develop. A widow for a couple of years should be about ready to have a man around the house.

We zipped along in Louise's Jag roadster until we were in the "burbs" with grand old homes and tree-lined streets. Once she patted my leg and let her fingers glide over the end of my large cock. "Possibilities just changed into definitely," I thought.

The Jag slowed and Louise turned into a long driveway that led to a large white house. It was something out of Hawthorne. Bric-a-brac and gables dominated the front with a large circular porch that wrapped itself around the front of the house. A two-door with leaded glass windows announced the entrance. We stopped in at a two-car garage and waited for the door to open. As we got out of the car, Louise began fishing around in her shoulder-strap purse. Finally, she found her keys. I noted her hand shook just a bit. I reached over, took the keys from her and unlocked the door, and stepped aside for her to enter first.

The interior of her house was a blend of Victorian and quiet comfort. After a tour of the first floor, she led me upstairs. We stopped at a large room with floor to ceiling windows that looked out into a spacious and beautifully landscaped backyard.

"How do you like this room?" Louise said.

"It's nice. Lots of space and I like space."

"The bathroom is directly across the hall. It has both a tub and a shower."

"How much?" I said as I let my hand caress my cock.

She noticed and let her gaze linger. I thought I caught a smile.

"Oh. Well—I haven't even thought about it."

"I notice you have a two stall garage. Would one be available for me to use? It would be nice to get my car off the street."

"Of course and the kitchen is yours to use, also."

"Great. When could I move in? The sooner the better as far as I'm concerned. The dorm drives me nuts," I said as I stretched just enough to tighten my pants to give her another look at my package.

"I guess today would be all right," Louise said. She felt a slight flush come over her and automatically place her hand on her face.

"Great. I need to call my father and let him know and have him clear it with the University's administration," I said as I pulled out my cell phone.

He must have been in a meeting because after the fourth ring he didn't pick up. I left him a message and my new address. Louise drove me back to my dorm so I could get my stuff and car. The Mercedes convertible didn't have a whole lot of room. It took three trips to get all of my gear to her house. As I entered the kitchen from the garage Louise said, "Dinner will soon be ready,"

"Wow! That's great. Sure smells good. Do I have time to shower?"

"Yes."

I went up to my room, carrying the last load of my stuff, stripped off my clothes, and walked across the hall to the bathroom. When I stepped out of the shower I realized there was only a hand-towel hanging on the rack. I dried off as best as I could and then returned to my room. I had a couple of clean towels stashed in one of my suitcases. While I was busy pulling out one of the suitcases from the close I didn't hear Louise come in. When I turned around she was standing there with an armful of towels.

"I'm so sorry, I forgot to put these in your bathroom," she said, her face red with embarrassment.

I walked over to her, still bare-ass naked, and took the towels from her. I openly looked her up and down appraising her. She blushed and didn't quite know what to do with herself. I finished drying myself, taking a bit longer as I handled my thickening cock.

"I have this aged bottle of wine that's begging to be opened. How about a glass before dinner?" I said as I strode over to a bookcase, picked up the bottle and two glasses. I felt her eyes on my butt.

I opened the bottle, poured two glasses, and walked over to her, and handed one to her.

"You always keep wine on hand?"

"Actually, no, I don't. It was a gift," I replied as I tipped my glass to hers and giving her my best open invitation to join me in bed.

Louise was too nervous to pick up my cue so I reached around her to a dresser for a pack of cigarettes. I let my cock rub against her. I offered her one. She declined. She seemed to be waiting. I guess for me to get my clothes on. That would not do.

"Look, Louise, you are hot and I want you to come to bed with me, right now."

"What?" She stammered. "I need to go . . ."

I stepped a bit closer, leaned forward, and nibbled on her ear, ran my tongue down her neck. Her lips parted and I kissed her, probing her mouth with my tongue. I pulled her closer to me and began a slow rhythmic movement of my hips against her.

"Davy," she said, paused, and then continued, "I—," I kissed her in mid-sentence.

I shot my hand up her dress. I realized she had no panties on. My middle finger found its home and as I gently massaged her mons, I knew she was mine. I picked her and carried her over to the bed. I shoved her dress up to expose her. Quickly, my tongue found her clit and I began a rapid massage. Soft groans synced with her push upward to meet the thrusts of my tongue. Her clit was firm and ready and so was I.

Her labia clung to my throbbing poker, caressing it, teasing it. She wrapped her legs around me, pulling her sweetness up to give me a better shot. I slowed my heated thrusts to an easy steady rhythm. Soon she began to moan and her lips parted as she gasped. Her whole body shivered as she reached her first orgasm. I felt a low rumble at the base of my cock as I slammed it to her. Volcano-like, I erupted as my sperm flew out of my thick tube. I felt my glans expand as it widened to allow my cock-fluid to flow.

I heard her whisper, "Oh, Davy. It's been so long."

"You feel better now?" I replied as I kissed her.

"Yes! Yes!"

"I asked her if she wanted more as I felt my cock harden.

She did. We spent the next three days in bed. There sure is something good to say about an older woman. She did whatever I wanted and came back for more. She was exceptional. I maintained a separate room just in case she had relatives come to visit or anyone else for that matter. Things were wonderful smooth in our lives."

But things were not to be. Toward the end of summer school, I got a phone call that changed everything. My father had a heart attack. I threw some clothes in a suitcase and took off. Louise had gone to work. I hurriedly scribbled a quick note for her and left."

He died before I got there," I said as I felt my heartbeat kick up a couple of notches.

"I'm sorry to have you bring up that sad moment in your life. Getting it out in the open will help you heal," P.J. interrupted.

"I didn't go back to school. The next two months were filled with legal stuff. My two brothers were each left $100,000 and I was left a half million; the bulk of the estate went to my mother."

"What about Louise?"

"I drove back to New Haven, stopped at Louise's. She was at work. I hadn't talked to her since I had left. I packed up the rest of my stuff, wrote her a note, and left. I've not talked to her or written to her," I said.

"And you feel no remorse about that?" P.J. asked.

"No. As far as I was concerned it was a summer's fling. I never made any commitment beyond staying there during my time at school."

"So, what did you do?"

"I took off for Sweden, entered a university, and buried myself in my studies. The emersion in philosophy helped me not to miss my father. I graduated and then moved to Madrid to work on an advanced degree. From there I went to India and completed my doctorate at the University of Hyderabad. From there, I journeyed to the mountains of Tibet and spent the next two years with the monks."

"That was a big junk of concentrated studies. What did you do after Tibet?"

"I went home. I found my mother had remarried. He was a well-to-do gentleman who spent his time making her happy. I liked him. I didn't stay there very long. I moved to New York and there took an active role in managing my financial affairs."

"So you liked New York?" P.J. asked.

"It kept me occupied. Then out of the blue, I began to think of Monte and Dawn. I made several trips to Canada. Each trip ended in disappointment. One of the assets I got when my father died was a twelve square mile tract of land he had purchased. Not sure how that all came about but anyway, I took to wandering around in the bush; camping our summer and winter. I lived off the land. It was during that time I wrote my first philosophy book.

Loneliness began to haunt me day and night. In desperation, I returned to the United States and that's when I called you."

"Truly, remarkable. I appreciate your candid sharing. It's been a long night. You need to get some rest before your trip north. I'll have you called in a few hours. That way you can begin the next part of your journey refreshed," P.J. said.

CHAPTER FIVE

Sleep covered me quickly and I slept until mid-afternoon. After a hearty lunch, I packed my bags, called for a rental to be delivered. P.J. was not around and Joseph did not indicate where he was. The rental arrived. I left a quick note for P.J. and headed north. I drove until early morning; pulled off to the side of the road and closed my eyes. Sleep was welcome.

I was awakened by a tapping on my car window. I struggled to get my eyes open. Clarity finally came and I recognized the uniform of the Royal Canadian Mounted Police. I rolled down the window.

"You Davy Fuchs?"

"Yes, officer. Is there a problem?

"Follow me in your car. I will explain later."

I did as he said. Several miles later we exited onto a dirt road and ended up at a small lake. I pulled to a stop and hopped out of my rental.

"Okay. Enough of this. Either you tell me what this is all about or I am out of here," I growled.

"A plane is about to land. It's here to pick you up to fly you back into the bush. You must have some very important friends in high places."

"I don't understand."

"You're headed north to the Reservation, are you not?"

102

"Yes, but—," The sound of a plane interrupted my statement.

Shortly a seaplane glided on to the smooth lake. A young, uniformed man climbed out on to one of the pontoons and shoved a small rubber boat into the water. Effortlessly, he paddled the short distance over to where we were standing. He jumped out of the boat and sauntered over to us.

"You must be Fuchs," he said looking at me.

"Yes. Who are you and who sent you?" I said still unhappy about the turn of events.

"Name's Rogers. The Secretary of the Interior sent me to take you to the Reservation."

Still not quite willing to accept all of this I said, "And who is this Secretary?"

"P.J. Saulo. I thought you knew."

"You mean Dr. P. J. Saulo, the psychiatrist?

"Yes sir."

It has never occurred to me that P.J. was a ranking senior government official. No wonder he could travel wherever he wanted. I shook my head knowing that P.J. was probably having a good laugh and at my expense.

"Any time you are ready, sir," Rogers said.

I tossed my gear into the skiff and we took off for the plane. Within minutes we were airborne and headed north to the Reservation. Two hours later we were landing. I had Rogers land on the backside of my little island. It looked very much the same as it did when I left it several years ago. I deposited my bags on the sandy beach and noticed a small black bag I knew was not mine.

"That's not mine," I said.

"Dr. Saulo wanted you to have it," Rogers replied. "He said it was important and I should make sure you got it."

"Thanks for the lift. Tell Dr. Paulo I will be in touch with him," I said as Rogers boarded his plane. As the plane took off, I waved and waited until it was out of sight. Then I picked up my gear and headed toward the small clearing I knew so well.

It was as it had been. I sat down on the small patch of grass and breathed in the smell of the place as the sun bathed me in its warmth. I felt at ease, the first in a long time. I got up and made camp; including storing my gar in one of the trees just to keep it safe from any prowling animals. I kept the small black bag. Once I had it open I had to laugh. It contained smoke and fire powders, solutions to change water to the color of blood, a couple of jars of salves, a box of itching powder, and one of sneezing powder. All stuff a small-time magician would use. P.J. understood the importance of showmanship.

Once I had got over my amusement, I set about building my camp. I quickly put up a lean-to, dug a fourteen-inch deep hole in the ground, and lined it with stones. This would be my cooking fire. I had time to go fishing for my supper and to have a quick swim. I speared a Great Northern Pike, gutted and scaled it, and then wrapped in nettle leaves. Started my fire, and waited for the stones to heat. Once they were hot, I placed the nettle-leaves wrapped Pike on the hot coals. Then I went for a quick swim. The

104

June sun had not as yet penetrated the lower depths of the lake and the water was icy cold. I was shivering as I clambered back up on the beach.

She was standing there. I made to attempt to cover my nakedness. She had had me in the past. She was the first to speak.

"You are even more handsome if that's possible."

"And you are as beautiful as ever," I replied.

"Why did you come back?" Dawn said.

"Because it is within the order of things."

"Order of things? What does that mean?"

"Yes. At least it is what Monte believed," I said as I made sure there was no emotion in my voice.

"Monte? I don't understand," Dawn said.

I caught the slight quiver of her lower lip.

"He wrote me just before his death," I replied and this time I set the coldness I felt toward her show in my voice.

"What? What did he tell you?"

"Much including the fact the two of you had broken up."

"You do know he killed himself, don't you?" Dawn asked.

"I know he did not kill himself. Suicide was not a part of his life's pattern."

Dawn's dark eyes darkened and filled with hate. She gasped as she noticed the medallion hanging around my neck and down my naked chest. Her hate turned to fear.

"Where—where did you get that?" Dawn said pointing at the medallion.

"That's not for you to know. Why did you stab Monte and kill him?"

"I—I didn't."

"Don't lie to me. You may hide the truth from the police and even your people, but not from me. I have read your evil thoughts and I know you are afraid and well you should be."

She lunged at me with a long-bladed knife. I slapped her aside and she fell. She quickly rolled over into a squat, knife still in her hand. A deep low growl filled the air. Thinking it was me; Dawn sprang to her feet and ran into the bush. A shrill horrified scream filled the air. I heard a loud crunch. The brush parted and the largest cinnamon bear I had ever seen rumbled into the clearing. It was dragging Dawn's limp bloody body. Seeing me, it dropped her and reared up on its hind legs. A terrifying growl filed the air challenging me.

I froze; even stopped breathing and because I did the huge bear stopped. That moment was all I needed. I grabbed a burning stick from my fire pit and swung it high in the air. Sparks flew and it burst into full flame. I rushed the bear, screaming at the top of my voice. It swung it huge pats at me and I ducked just in the nick of time. As I did so, I shoved the burning stick into its stomach. Burnt hair filled the air. The bear was on fire and in a wild rage, it plunged past me and rushed headlong back through the bush.

Instantly, flames shot up. The sudden fire brought me to action. I was about to be trapped. Grabbing the black bag and my luggage, I ran to the

106

edge of the lake and jumped in. Because the luggage floated I had a small raft to cling to. The night was made daylight by the roaring flames as they swept over what was once my little paradise. A lonely sadness filled me as I realized my two friends were dead and now so was the place I once loved; my private world was in flames. Slowly I began to kick my way out into deeper water and headed toward the mainland.

Noise from the mainland brought me back from remembering what it was like fucking Dawn. I could see many figures running around. The Indians were watching the flamed island with natural concern. A slight shift in the wind could bring hot sparks to their small village and they, like the island would be in flames. I swam toward them.

When I stood up out of the water several women screamed and small children cried out. All of them stepped back and huddled in fear. I suppose it was nerve-racking especially since I towered over them, my nakedness, and the flames on the islands a backdrop. I climbed out of the water and up the sandy bank and stood before them. No one moved or spoke to me. Finally, one from among them stepped forward; an old man with long white hair. I waited for him to speak.

He spotted the medallion that hung down from my neck. He opened his mouth to speak but no sounds came out. Suddenly, he dropped to the ground and on his knees; he bowed to me three times. I extended my hand to him and pulled him up.

"There is no need for you to kneel. Take me to the teepee of death."

The old man looked at me; his mouth agape, with horror-filled eyes. Finally, he gained enough courage to speak.

"It is filled with evil. She who remains brings sickness to all of my people. Why do you want to go there?"

Speaking loud enough for all to hear, I said, "It is the place where my friend, Monte was murdered. I want to cleanse the area. His murderer is no longer. She tried to kill me. She is no more." I pointed back toward the burning island.

The old man's eyes widened. I looked down at him and smiled as I placed my hand on his shoulder. I felt his body quiver. He wanted to flee. I continued to hold his gaze and the trembling and fear quieted itself. Turning he walked back toward the small village. I followed him as did the rest of those who had gathered. Dogs set up a howling; some growled as we approached. One particularly mean snarling dog rushed at me. I stopped, stood still, and held out my hand. It slid to a halt, whimpered, and rolled over on its back waiting for a death blow. I scratched its belly and walked on.

The old one pointed to a large teepee. He refused to go any further. I casually strolled over to the tent. Excitement filled me as I pulled back the flap. I wasn't sure what I expected to find. It took a few seconds for my eyes to adjust to the dark. My skin crawled as I felt a presence. A bright blaze filled the tent revealing a smiling old woman looking at me.

"I am grandmother of Monte, he who was killed by the she-witch," she said in broken French and English.

"How do you know that?" I whispered.

"He told me as he lay dying. I am the one who sent you the medallion and the letter to you. It was his last wish."

"Thank you Old One," I said. "Do you know why Dawn killed Monte?"

"Some things are best left with the dead," she replied.

"You recognize the power of this medallion. You cannot deny me," I said with just a touch of a growl in my voice.

She looked at me, eyes wide and filled with fear. Her deep-wrinkled face grayed. Then hesitatingly she said, "Gold. She killed him for gold."

"Gold," I questioned. "Continue," I said.

"There is a mountain of gold many moons' walk from here. I am the only one who can read the signs painted on these walls," she said with a sweeping gesture across the inner walls of the teepee.

I picked up a small branch, held it in the hot coals of the small fire. It soon caught and as I held it up high above our heads I saw many drawings.

"She killed him because he refused to tell her what they meant. She didn't know he couldn't because I am the only one who knows."

"And now you will reveal their meanings to me," I said.

She pointed to one section of the teepee on which was many drawings. Slowly, she began to tell me the story of each picture, and as she talked I suddenly realized it located on a tract of land I owned about fifty miles due north of where were presently were. I began to recognize landmarks and realized the mountain she was talking about was one I had camped on years ago.

"Green is evil," she said and then stopped talking.

"Was Monte aware of—."

She cut me off: "You need food and drink."

She left me standing there. I squatted down, added a few small pieces of wood to the small fire, and systematically memorized each berry-stained image. My mind went into racetrack mode thinking about all that wealth could do for these people.

"Hmm, I wonder if Dawn killed Monte in here, and if so if his blood still stains the ground."

The Old One soon returned with a basket of pemmican and maple syrup. She placed a pot filled with water on the smoldering embers. Noticing my look, she said, "Birch tea. Good for you."

She squatted near the fire and watched me eat. Once the water boiled she emptied a bunch of chopped birch bark into the water, stirred it around, and poured some in a metal cup. I nodded and said thank you as I shoved the remaining meat over to her and indicated she should eat. She got up and rummaged around soon retrieved another cup and filled it with some of the tea. We sat in silence as she ate and I drank my tea.

Breaking the silence, the Old One asked, "You have a woman?"

"No, I'm not married."

"You need woman. I come back," she said openly looking at my cock.

Before I could protest, she was gone. A disgusting thought seized me. "Good god, she wants to sleep with me. How am I going to get out of this?"

A huge roar and screaming broke my thoughts. I stepped outside and women and children were running. Men were shouting and dogs were barking and growling. Torches had been lighted. It was then I saw it. The bear, the same one that had killed Dawn was swiping at everyone. One of the bolder dogs was decapitated by an effortless swipe from its mammoth paws. Another dog's body went flying through the air. One of the men rushed the bear. It grabbed him and rushed him with its huge gaping mouth. His lifeless body fell to the ground. The bear reared up on its hind feet. Now nearly nine feet tall, it swayed its front paws back and forth as a way to ward off any attackers. I realized it had only one eye.

I dashed back into the teepee and searched for a weapon. I could find none. I then remembered the black bag. I opened it, pulled out a bottle of potassium, and ran back outside. The bear sensed my presence and let out a deafening roar. It lumbered toward me with its gigantic paws swaying back and forth. Fear seized me and I wanted to run. Slowly and with great caution, I inched my way toward the angry beast. Its huge body made me feel very small, nearly helpless. In the torchlight provided by the tribe, I could see its saliva dripping from its open mouth.

"It's now or never," I thought as I ran screaming toward the bear. I circled it and with each circle, I threw the potassium at it. With each circle it whirled, trying to face me. In a maddening rage, it lunged at me. I felt its hot breath as I jumped aside. I had used up the fiery chemical and it had not exploded into flames. Unsure of what to do next, I continued to run around the crazed beast yelling and waving my arms at it. Then it exploded into a mass of flames. The potassium had finally exploded.

Screams of terror filled the air as people ran every which way to escape the howling bear. Dogs with their tails between their legs fled. People had dropped their torches. I was very much alone with the desperate bear that continued to beat at its face to put out the fire and to stop the burning. The smell of burnt hair and flesh was sickening. I backed away from the horrible creature.

Someone stepped out from the shadows and thrust a bow and arrow into my hand. Quickly, I strung it, carefully aimed, and then let it fly. I heard the taunt string of the bow as it vibrated. The bear staggered, stood very still for a moment, and then toppled to the ground. I waited. Even in death throws an animal can rear up and kill you. I grabbed a bucket of water, threw it on the burning bear. The water sassed back at me; a protest for being put to such use. The fire went out and I was left in only the light of the night sky.

I heard movement and readied myself for another battle. The bear may have had its mate with it. Flashes of light broke the darkness as torches were again lit. Dozens of dancing, clapping, and laughing figures surrounded me. They stopped, dropped to their knees, and bowed down until their heads touched the earth.

"I was only protecting myself. Please get up," I said in a half-whisper.

One by one they stood and stepped before me, surrounded me, and upon some unspoken signal, the entire village began to dance and chant. The circle widened and then narrowed as they moved back and forward. Once again, they stopped, and an old man stepped into the circle and stood before me.

"Come. I have something for you," the man said.

Assuming he was the chief, I followed him to a teepee. Inside I smelt dried animal meat, dogs, and decaying animal skins He stuck his torch in the ground, knelt, and began digging. Soon, he came up with a small box tightly wrapped in oiled animal skin. Carefully, he removed the wrapping and gently opened the box. He removed a small pouch. He handed it to me and indicated I should open it. I did and my eyes nearly popped out of their sockets. It was a large uncut emerald. A quick guess made it at least 50 karats. I looked at him.

"It is yours. It has been handed down from my father's father, and those before him. It is my gift to you. You saved my people."

"But had it not been for me you and your people would not have been threatened by that bear," I said.

"Still, you risked your life. Besides, my grandson loved you."

"You are Monte's grandfather. It is my honor, sir. I should be giving you a gift."

"You have. You got rid of the Sea-Devil."

I replied. "Do you know what this is and what its value is?"

"It's of little value to me. I no longer have a grandson to pass it to. I am old and my time draws closer to its end. You are young and I will bring you much," the Chief replied.

"Tell me Old One, where are Monte's parents?"

"They are no longer."

The Chief's tone said it was not a topic for further questions. I placed the emerald back into the leather bag and then back into the box.

"Come, we eat now," the Chief said motioning me to follow him.

Most of the men were already drunk and had been gorging themselves on bear meat. Some were vomiting. It was a disgusting scene. I sat down with the Chief. He offered me some of the bear meat and a bottle of rot-gut whiskey. I declined the whiskey and nibbled on the meat. It was tough and had a strong taste. A number of the men curled up and went to sleep. The Chief dozed and I quietly got up and returned to what was now my teepee.

I was beat. My body ached. I wanted to be left alone. The death of my two friends grieved me and that sadness filled my heart. Sleep finally took hold of me and held me in its healing grip until midafternoon. The soft murmuring of people had stirred me awake. I was hungry and thirsty. I walked out into the clearing. My nakedness caused some of the women to stop their work. A few clucked as I walked by them. My duffle bag of clothes had been lost in the lake. I saw some water in a wooden keg with a hanging wooden dipper. I took a long slow drink. My nudity would have to wait until I had a swim. The truth is I enjoyed being naked. The difference now is there are more than just Monte and Dawn and me. I waded into the lake and let its water wash over me. As I came up for air, two young men in a canoe, paddled by me, waving, and shouting. I wasn't sure what they were saying. One of them reached down and brought up my duffle bag. I waved at them and shouted thanks.

I swam back to shore and clambered up the sandy bank. The two young men greeted me and handed me my duffle bag. I returned to my tent, opened the bag. My stuff on the bottom was soaking wet and things closer to the top were damp. It would take some time for everything thing to air dry. I took my clothes and went outside and began placing them on the ground. The Old Woman was there, had a fire going, and was cooking something.

"No bear meat," I said as I nodded my head at her.

She had prepared corn mash with honey and some very strong root tea. The mash was delicious but the tea was, as they say, was strong enough to kill a horse. Like before, she just walked off only this time she returned quickly. She handed me a loincloth. It barely covered my cock, but it worked.

"Thank you, Old One. Thank you for the food. You are very kind."

She smiled and then left me. I went into the teepee, opened the flaps, and systematically began to throw out stuff. Old blankets were shaken and taken down to the lake for a good soaking and then I began to beat them with stones to get them clean. My "woman's" activity caused quite a stir among the men as I spread the blankets on the grass to dry. I dug a new fire pit and lined it with stones. Once I had these things done, I went in search of the Chief.

I asked him if the Indian Agent Morand was in the area. He was and was at his summer place at the other end of the lake. I wanted to get a message out to Rogers, my pilot, and to the Secretary of Indian Affairs. I also asked for the hide of a large deer so I could cover myself. I thanked him for his help and then walked out to a large rock. It was quite flat on its top and I lay down to enjoy the warmth of the late afternoon soon. I must have dosed for I felt the change in the temperature. The sun was setting. I hurried back to my teepee. The Old One was waiting for me. Somehow I had to set her straight about being my woman.

Looking at me through squinted eyes she said, "You need woman. I brought you woman."

"What?" I replied.

"Inside. She will be your woman. Be gentle with her. She is young," she said and turned and walked away.

I pulled the teepee flap the rest of the way open and stepped in. Standing before the small fire in the center of the teepee was a totally beautiful young woman. Long shimmering black hair flowed down over her right breast. Both were perfectly shaped. Her liquid dark eyes reflected the glowing embers of the fire. Her lips slightly apart were so inviting. I felt a movement beneath my loincloth. I wanted her.

I smiled at her and she returned it with a timid smile; warm but not openly welcoming. Instinctively, I looked for resemblances to her mother. Curiously, there were none. Nor did I see any resemblance to Monte.

"Who are you?" I asked.

"I am the daughter of my father . . ."

"Don't lie to me. You are not Monte's daughter.

"Of course not. My father was He-Who-Walks-Far.

"Was?" I said as I felt my face flush.

"Yes, he is no more."

"And your mother?" I asked, trying to regain my composure.

"She died a few years after I was born. The Old One took me in and raised me as her own."

117

"I see. I thought you were the daughter of my two friends."

"The She-Devil could not have babies."

"I didn't know," I said as I squatted down next to the small fire. I moved my loincloth just a bit to give her a few a better view of my thickening club.

She handed me a bowl and said, "Eat." She moved to another part of the teepee.

I motioned for her to come and sit beside me. I offered her my bowl. She moved back from me.

"I mustn't," she said.

"Even if I insist," I said as I patted the spot next to me.

I dipped a chunk of the bread into the bowl filled with a stew and placed it near her lips.

"Please," I said.

She took one small bite and I did the same. We finished the bowl one small bite at a time.

"You have not told me your name," I said as I traced her lips with my finger.

"I am called Natasha."

"And I am Davy," I said leaning in closer to her. She smelled like fresh flowers.

"I know," she whispered.

She got up, prepared my bed of blankets by first softening the earth with grass. A soft animal skin was placed at the head as a pillow. Turning to me she said, "You like?"

"Yes, very much."

"Good. We go to bed now and you make me a woman," Natasha said as she dropped her dress.

118

I moved over to the fresh-made bed, dropped my loincloth, and lay down. She stretched out beside me and snuggled in close. Her lovely body sent pulsating shivers up and down my spine and my hungry cock. Her long fingers played a game on my chest and with each widening circle, she moved further down flat stomach until she was in my mass of blond hair that nested my club. She twirled my pubic hair around her fingers. Her play delighted me and my desire grew.

Finally, she got up enough courage to touch my expanded cock. It stood up, fully stiff, and very excited. It bobbed a manly bow. Fascinated, Natasha thumbed the smooth glans of my throbbing shaft. Her breathing quickened as she shot her warm tongue around my cock head. I gently kissed her as I rubbed each of her firm nipples. I slid my hand down along her thigh and moved it to her silken mons and gently rubbed it. I gradually added pressure as I continued my fevered kissing. Her labia opened and I shoved my middle finger deep into her virgin slit. I teased her clit and it budded. Small whimpering came from her as she moistened.

My hot kisses fell, lightning upon her sweet breasts. I kissed my way down her belly, pushed her legs further apart with my hand, and set my eager tongue to work sucking her clit. Her breathing quickened and her groaning grew louder. I eased myself up from her delicious young cunt, spread her legs even further apart, and aimed my pounding shaft into her wet canal.

I shoved downward and she exploded into her first orgasm. Her moisture made deeper penetration easier and with a forceful thrust, I destroyed her delicate membrane which protected her now defenseless womb. I wanted to slam into her but I fought the urge, steadied my strokes and my cock plowed deeper into her now very swollen cunt.

Her lips were slightly parted and her eyes were closed.

"Open your eyes and look at me," I whispered. I got up from her so she could see my cock and balls.

Natasha smiled as her cheeks flushed. She reached out, cupped my balls and then my cock. I spread her legs and plunged back into her. I rotated my hips and then shoved my cock from one side to the other of her eager clit.

"Like it?" I asked as I panted and tried to catch my breath. I felt the sweat trickle down my sides.

"Yes. It's wonderful. We made baby. It is good."

"I don't know. Time will tell," I said as I lay my long semi-hard cock along her thigh.

The idea of fatherhood felt good. I had not considered that possibility for a long time. "Yes," I thought, "It is good."

We stayed in bed for the next three days; getting up only to relieve ourselves. I taught her how to sit on my hard hot poker and to ride it up and down. Her appetite for my cock was endless. In total ecstasy, she sucked my cock dry. If she wasn't knocked up, it wasn't because I didn't feed her enough cock juice. I emerged on the morning of the fourth day. I went down to the lake and dove in. Its cold waters refreshed me. With the one bar of soap, I had salvaged from my duffle bag, I lathered my balls and cock and armpits. Rinsed and swam back to the shore. I picked up my loincloth; spoke to one of the young men about borrowing a canoe, shoved it into the water and as I headed out I waved to Natasha. I headed for the Morand place.

It was a large log house. The Canadian flag flapped back and forth in a light breeze. Morand spotted me and came to the edge of the water to greet me. I was still naked. It seemed to embarrass him. I slipped on my loincloth and climbed up the sandy bank.

"Hello, Davy. Good god, man, what happened to your clothes? Don't tell me you've gone native."

"Burned up on the island fire a little over a week ago," I replied.

We continued to exchange pleasantries as we walked to his house. Once inside food was served. It tasted good after eating dried caribou.

"So, Davy, what can I do for you?" Morand said as he sipped the last of his wine.

"I want you to contact Rogers and have him fly in and pick me up. My business here is finished. On my property to the north of here, there is a gold mine. I want to give it to the local tribe. Here are the directions and the mine's exact location," I said handing him a folded piece of paper.

121

"Are you talking about the rumored hidden mine? If so, you realize it is just a rumor. Men have died searching for it," Morand said.

"I am aware of the rumors. However, I am confident this is real and I want them to have the right to mine the gold but no ownership of the property. They are to have legal access."

"But do you know this is the real thing?"

"The map was etched into Monte's teepee. It just looked like a design. His grandmother explained it to me when she realized I was now wearing the shaman's medallion that had belonged to Monte. Will you do this for me?"

"Of course," Morand replied.

"Thank you. I want to talk with Dr. Saulo. May I use your short wave radio?"

"You'll have to wait until morning. No one mans the office at night. You are very welcome to stay here."

I realized the sun had dipped behind the mountains and even though I knew how to travel at night there was still the possibility of the dead bear's mate being around.

"Thank you. Are you sure it won't be an inconvenience? I notice you have a new housekeeper."

"She is the sister of the one you know. She and my wife are off to be with our daughter who is having a baby. Hopefully, they will be back in a couple of days," Morand said as he heaved a sigh.

"You are sure it's not too much for me to stay over? "

"No trouble. You can sleep in the girl's bed and she can sleep in the kitchen by the warm stove. We have a cot that she can set up."

We had a brandy and then retired. The feel of the soft bed beneath me felt good and the smell of clean white sheets along with being in a house again filled me with pleasant contentment. I stretched out full length and let out a very satisfied groan. The bedroom door opened. It was the housekeeper.

"I heard a groan. Are you okay?" She whispered as she stepped into the room.

"I'm fine. Come and sit beside me and tell me about you," I said as I patted a spot on the bed.

She carefully shut the door and came and sat on the edge of my bed. I was naked and had no bed covers over me. Moonlight filled my room with a soft glow and she could easily see my large cock. Slowly her hand slid along my leg.

"Are you sure you are okay?" She said as she wrapped her fingers around my thickening cock. I reached over and pulled her down. She did not resist my kisses. I pulled up her cotton nightgown and began to gently rub her mons. She spread her legs and I rolled into her. With a quick shove of throbbing dick, my glans found its mark. She pushed against me eager to take all of me in. Happily, I reamed away until she hit her peak and burst into a full orgasm. I continued to pound away are her open slit until I shot my load. I withdrew my cock and rolled over onto my back. She started to get up.

"Not yet," I said. "Lie down between my legs and suck my cock."

She gulped me down. Her lips flew up and down my bulging shaft bringing me to a boil. I held her head and shoved. She swallowed and had my cock down her throat taking all of my juice. She stayed until just before dawn. She slipped out of bed and returned to the kitchen.

Breakfast was a feast of bacon, eggs, fried potatoes, and real toast. The coffee, real coffee, was wonderful. I hadn't realized how much I missed certain things in a more civilized setting. I felt wonderful. I radioed P.J. and let him know I would be returning to Toronto. The morning sun was perfect. I paddled my way back to the Indian encampment. There I packed my gear and once again tried to give the emerald to the Old One. Again, he refused saying it was written that I should have it.

The plane glided across the smooth water and came to a halt a few yards offshore. Rogers waved and I waved back. It was quite something to see the villagers lined up to wave goodbye. Natasha stood among them, head lowered. I stowed my gear and a few gifts into the rubber raft and with a shove and a jump I was in the raft and headed toward the plane. I looked up to wave goodbye. Natasha did not wave. With a roar, the engine came to life and we were speeding across the lake and then lifted into the air.

"Turn around. Go back!" I yelled.

"What the fuck? I've got a schedule to meet."

"Do as I say or you will never fly a plane again. Now turn around and go back."

The floatplane glided to a stop. I threw the rubber raft into the water and hopped in. With a few swift strokes with the single paddle, I was onshore. I raced up the sandy bank. Sometimes I slipped in the sand and fell. I clawed my to the top and panting stood in front of Natasha. I grabbed her in my arms, slung her over my shoulders, and jump-leaped my way back down the bank. With little effort, I tossed her into the raft and then climbed in. We were soon at the plane, boarded, and ready to take off.

With a roar, the engines revved up and we were soon airborne.

Instead of sitting with the piolet, I sat in the back, holding Natasha close to me. I felt her tremble. It wasn't fright but more excitement. I kissed her on her forehead and stroked her soft black hair.

"I could not leave you. I will never leave you. We, you and me, are one," I whispered in her ear.

I felt tears tumble down my face. I'm not sure if they were hers or mine.

She moved and eased herself onto my lap. With a quick jerk, my fly was open and I freed my throbbing cock. With ease, she slid her eager mons down my shaft. I wrapped my arms around her, kissed her letting my tongue explore her sweet mouth. I felt my juices come to a boil and with a shove, I exploded deep within her warm moist cunt.

125

She leaned against me and went to sleep.

Two hours later we landed at the *Hydro Aéroport de Montréal*. A chauffeur-driven stretch limo was waiting on the dock. The uniformed driver approached us.

"Sir, are you Dr. Fuchs?"

"Yes," I replied.

"I'm to drive you to the *Trudeau International* Airport. Your plane is waiting for you, Sir."

Natasha and I slid into the limo and we were soon speeding through the streets of Montréal. We boarded a Dassault Falcon 8X, totally luxurious inside. Of course we took advantage of joining the "fight club" and had extended sex in one of the two bedrooms on board the plane.

CHAPTER SIX

"So, from the Canadian bush you returned to the States. How did your mother react to your bringing home an Indian woman?" P.J. asked as he leaned forward with renewed interest in my story.

"She accepted Natasha but did insist we be married in a church. We had no issue with that. Natasha insisted we also include her Indian name in the ceremony."

"And what was that? You've not told me her Native name?" P.J. replied.

"Her name—," I paused—"My god, I thought, "have I blocked her that far out of my life?"

"Davy, you are drifting off again. What was Natasha's Native name?" J.P. asked. His voice was sharp.

"What? Oh, it was Shining Star," I said and I began sobbing.

P.J. handed me a tissue.

"Sorry, Doc. She was the only woman I can honestly say I loved," I said wiping my eyes.

"You said Shining Star told you that the two of you 'made a baby.' Tell me about your child?

"Nine months later she went into labor. That's when everything went to hell. She screamed just once and stopped breathing. They couldn't revive her. The doctors did a C-section immediately. Our son was dead. Natasha was dead."

"Were you ever told the cause of their deaths? If so, what was the cause?"

"There was a massive rupture of an artery within the womb. She bled to death and our son drowned."

"As horrific as that was, you cannot blame yourself," P.J. said as he reached out and patted me on the shoulder.

"But I do," I cried. "I do."

"Why?"

"I—I fucked her the night before." I screamed at P.J. "I caused a uterine rupture and my son suffocated and Natasha bled to death. How in hell can you expect me to get over that?"

"Certainly not by trying to amputate your penis," P.J. replied. "You have an obligation to Natasha, a very serious obligation."

"What?" "Shit, I thought you was a real shrink. You're no better than the others," I said.

"Such a temper, Davy, and in front of your son," Merida said as she and a one-year-old blond haired boy entered the office.

"I—I didn't know," I stammered as he ran over to me and climbed up on my lap. "I didn't know." Tears streamed down my face. "What's your name?" I managed to ask.

"Davy, Davy Fuchs."

"And so I do," I thought.

THE END

128

www.ingramcontent.com/pod-product-compliance
Lightning Source LLC
Chambersburg PA
CBHW011516170626
46810CB00009B/3383